Avenging Angels

'Kneel down and lie across the phone table,' she told him, once he stood naked but for his shirt and tie in front of her.

The surge of power which rushed through her veins as he obeyed made Karen feel exultant. Aaron's buttocks looked very white against the red velour of the telephone seat. Leaning forward, Karen ran her fingertip from his waist to the bottom of his spine, noting how his buttocks clenched as she reached the beginning of his cleft. She smiled to herself.

'This will never do,' she said softly, 'not if you want me to let you come. And you do want me to let you come, don't you Aaron?' she crooned.

'Bitch!' Aaron said between his teeth, though his voice quivered, betraying his excitement.

Avenging Angels

ROXANNE CARR

BLACK
lace

Black Lace novels are sexual fantasies.
In real life, make sure you practise safe sex.

First published in 1997 by
Black Lace
332 Ladbroke Grove
London W10 5AH

Typeset by CentraCet, Cambridge
Printed and bound by Mackays of Chatham PLC

ISBN 0 352 33147 X

Prologue

*H*e was waiting for her when she came out of the meeting of new holidaymakers which she had just addressed. Leaning on an old moped, his bright blue shirt open at the neck, dark glasses obscuring the expression in his eyes, he looked mean and moody, unapproachable. He smiled, though, as she reached him.

'Ricardo! What are you doing here?' Karen could feel the heat creeping under her skin and cursed her English complexion for betraying her. No matter how cool she managed to act, he could always tell how she felt by observing the blush on her cheeks.

'I was waiting for you. You are free now, yes?'

She glanced back at the gaggle of tourists meandering out of the lobby of the hotel. One of them might want a word with her.

'Well, I . . .'

'We could go to the beach – a little beach I know near my father's house. No tourists.'

Karen gazed at him, aware of him with all her senses – of the warmth of his skin, the strength of his hand as he reached out to touch her face. Slowly, he removed his sunglasses, and she found herself drowning, drowning in eyes the colour of liquid milk chocolate.

'I suppose I could,' she whispered, oblivious now to the curious glances of the holidaymakers who were passing them.

Ricardo grinned, flashing impossibly straight, white teeth at her, and straddled the scooter. Hitching up her short, white skirt, Karen slung her duffle bag over her shoulder, climbed on behind him and slipped her arms around his waist. She felt his abdominals ripple as he kick-started the scooter and, without thinking about what she was doing, she splayed her fingers across his stomach as they pulled away, pressing herself tightly against his back as they moved off.

She'd met him days after arriving in Tierra del Sol, when he'd come to deliver a promotional flyer to the hotel where she was based. From the moment their eyes had met, Karen had felt a spark, an actual *frisson* between them. It had been so powerful that, when he had leant across the counter she had been keeping between them and asked her to meet him after work, she had overcome her natural shyness and said yes.

Karen smiled now as they hurtled along the winding coast road, and pressed her cheek against his back. It hadn't taken Ricardo long to realise that

2

she was still a virgin, nor for her to realise that this somehow made her rise in his estimation of her. He hadn't pressurised her like the boys back home had done, respecting, even approving of, her desire to wait for someone truly special.

Instead he had wooed her with soft words and even softer caresses, making her want him slowly, gradually, until lately she could think of nothing but how it would be when they finally made love.

Karen had no doubt in her mind that they would, eventually, sleep together, for over the past few months she had fallen deeply in love with Ricardo. She trusted him and was, at last, ready to take that final step into womanhood. She wanted, more and more, to signal that readiness to him, to show him that she believed him to be the special man she had always been waiting for, but she didn't know how, and for once she cursed her inexperience.

The warm breeze caressed her face as they rounded the bend and she closed her eyes as a cloud of red dust billowed under the scooter's wheels. Beneath her hands, she could feel the contours of Ricardo's body, the flesh warm and supple, the muscles sculpted delicately between skin and bone.

There was no doubt about it, he was utterly gorgeous. Karen had seen the way other girls looked at him and was proud to be the one he had chosen to have on his arm all summer long. Being this close to him, she felt her own skin tingle, and hitherto unexplored feelings churned in the pit of her stomach as she felt her inner flesh pulse gently in anticipation, the tender channels growing slick with moisture.

They skidded to a halt in a cloud of red sand.

'We'll leave the bike here,' he told her as she climbed off.

Her legs felt weak for a moment, and she reached out to steady herself with her hand against his shoulder. Ricardo covered it with his own and she felt the strength of his fingers as they closed over hers. A curious fluttering sensation in the pit of her stomach kept her immobile as he took her hand and lifted it to his lips. His eyes held hers as he kissed the back of it, their message unreadable.

'We – we'd better get down to the beach,' she stammered, suddenly feeling unsure of herself.

There was something so – so worldly about the way Ricardo was looking at her, and she suddenly felt afraid. He sensed it, and smiled, drawing her close.

'What is it, my darling?' he asked her softly, his hands stroking her back through the thin cotton of her blouse.

Karen felt very young and rather foolish. 'It's nothing,' she said, attempting to laugh it off.

But Ricardo would not be fooled. 'I will look after you . . . always,' he said.

Karen looked at him in surprise, standing acquiescent as he untied her ponytail and brought her long, dark hair up to his face. He stroked a tress of it across his cheek in a gesture so sensuous it made her catch her breath.

God, she wanted him! She tried to tell him with her eyes – it wasn't that she didn't trust him, only

4

that she was afraid of the unknown, of her ability to please him . . .

'Come – we can swim, yes?' He spoke and the moment passed.

'All right.'

She smiled, half disappointed that his mood seemed to have lightened, half relieved that they seemed to be back on their familiar easy-going footing.

To get to the beach they had to climb down a long, winding path which narrowed in places to a mere foot's width. Karen could see why the beach didn't attract many tourists – from the top of the cliff it was impossible to see what lay below.

Unlike the south of the island, where most of the tourist development was situated, this coastline was rugged, the beaches bordered by cliffs. As they climbed, a gull wheeled overhead, squawking as if outraged at their presence. Ricardo, walking in front of her, looked back and grinned as he caught her eye.

That grin warmed and reassured her. As she made her way to the base of the cliffs, Karen had a growing sense of something momentous about to happen. Her entire body seemed to be tingling with awareness, primed by Ricardo's long and patient courtship. She was excited, yet apprehensive. Not liking to be too far away from him, she hurried to catch up, earning herself a quizzical glance as she bumped into him.

'Careful, darling, – we are on a precipice here.'

Karen read significance into his choice of words and slipped her hand into his. He squeezed it briefly, smiling at her as she jumped down the incline on to the pale, soft sand.

Catching her breath, she looked around her. They were standing in a small, semi-circular bay, sheltered by the towering cliffs which also provided a little shade. The virgin sand was pure and clean, washed daily by the tide. Now the iridescent sea lapped gently at the shoreline some several metres away. Karen could smell the sweet saltiness of the air, and she took a deep breath, filling her lungs with it.

'Oh, Ricardo!' she breathed. 'It's beautiful.'

'Yes, it is beautiful,' he said, though as she turned to face him, she saw that he was looking, not at the view, but at her.

He smiled at her discomfiture. 'Let's swim,' he said.

Karen watched him as he pulled off his T-shirt, admiring the way his muscles rippled beneath the smooth, golden skin. A smattering of dark hair already patterned his chest, and she guessed it would grow thicker as he matured. His body was a clear signal of what he would become, and Karen found herself wondering if she might see the attractive boy she loved turn into the handsome man she believed he would be.

Catching her looking at him, he smiled, but said nothing, holding her gaze as he unfastened his jeans and peeled them down his legs. He was wearing plain black swimming trunks underneath, not miniscule and blatantly revealing, but a snug fit, outlining the strong, straight shape of his penis underneath.

Karen dragged her eyes away, suddenly bemused as she realised he knew she was looking at him. Covering her embarrassment, she reached into her bag for her bikini. No more than three triangles of red fabric, threaded on to strings of black nylon, Karen suddenly felt reluctant to change into it. It was ridiculous – Ricardo had seen her in the bikini countless times and she had never given it a thought. Somehow, though, she knew their relationship had undergone a subtle alteration, and she felt self-conscious with him for the first time.

'Come on!' he chivvied her, his dark eyes dancing with amusement.

When he made no move to look away, Karen made a face at him.

'You go on – I'll catch up with you.'

Something flashed across his eyes, something dark and illicit which sent a thrill shivering up her spine. Then it was gone and he turned away.

Karen watched him running, light-footedly, across the sand towards the shoreline, as she waited for her heart to stop racing. Slowly, she changed into the tiny bikini, before dumping her bag and clothes next to his.

The sand was hot beneath her feet as she ran to join him, the water silky-cool over her skin. She felt him watching her as she waded towards him, assessing and admiring her exposed body. Her skin seemed to tingle as his eyes caressed it, making her feel hot and bemused in spite of the coolness of the water. Diving beneath the surface to hide her confusion, she swam underwater towards him, catching him off balance so that he lost his footing and sank down to join her.

They broke the surface of the water together, laughing. Ricardo shook his head so that his wet hair was flung back from his face, and pulled her into his arms. The look in his eyes made Karen tremble afresh, and she gasped as his mouth claimed hers.

His lips tasted of sea salt as they moved on hers, and Karen instinctively ran her tongue along their inner edges, opening her mouth to him. She felt rather than heard him groan, the vibration meeting the trembling in her own throat, and melding with it until she couldn't be sure which reaction was his and which her own.

Confused for a moment, she broke the kiss and swam away, from him. She was a strong swimmer, her arms cutting powerfully through the water, yet even so, he caught up with her in no time. They swam in silence for some time, side by side, front crawl one way, backstroke to return.

After a while, Karen began to tire. Rolling on to her front, she struck out for the shore with a more leisurely breaststroke. Ricardo followed suit. Still he was silent, though Karen was again conscious of his eyes on her as they both walked out of the water and up the beach.

'Here.' He spread two towels side by side on the pale sand and Karen sank gratefully on to one of them. Closing her eyes, she steadied her breathing, waiting quietly for the racing of her heart to settle.

When she opened her eyes, she found that

Ricardo was propped up on one elbow on the other towel, watching her.

'What?' she said. 'What is it?'

He smiled, a small, enigmatic smile that made her mouth turn dry. He picked up a tress of her long, dark hair and wound it around his fingers.

'With such dark hair you could almost be Spanish,' he said unexpectedly. 'It's so unusual with such pale skin.'

'Irish ancestry,' Karen replied, aware that her voice quivered. 'On my mother's side.'

'That would explain your eyes, then.'

'My eyes?'

'Aren't Irish eyes supposed to smile?'

'You've heard that song?'

He grinned at her. 'I keep my eyes and ears open around the tourists; I see and hear many things. But I've never seen eyes as violet as yours.'

'Oh? Have you gazed into many?'

Her attempt to lighten the tone was a failure. He was moving closer to her, his head dipping to allow him to brush his lips, soft as the kiss of a butterfly's wing, across her temples.

Karen's eyes closed of their own volition, their lids weighted by an emotion she recognised, but didn't quite understand. Ricardo's lips touched them lightly before moving down her nose to her parted lips.

'You taste of sea and sunshine,' he murmured, his voice as rich and soft as velvet.

A warmth which had little to do with the sun seeped through her body as his tongue probed gently at the barrier of her teeth. With a small sigh, she surrendered to him, snaking her arms around his neck and moulding the upper half of her body to his.

His hair, made still darker by the sea, was slicked back on his head, like a seal's coat. The outline of his face was clearly defined, its contours strong and sharp. Karen felt a rush of love for him so intense she gasped aloud.

Enfolded in his arms, Karen felt soft and weightless, intensely feminine. His chest was hard and unyielding, a wall against which her breasts flattened, and her heartbeat battered against his.

He had kissed her before, of course, many times, but this time she sensed in him an urgency, a need that he had never allowed her to see before now.

'Ricardo . . .'

'Ssh,' he whispered, pressing his fingertips against her lips. 'Trust me, my darling. I will not hurt you . . . only love you. You do want me to love you, don't you?'

Karen gazed up at him, aware that the clamour of her senses was drowning out the voice of reason which had held her back until now. Her lips moved soundlessly, her eyes widening into two liquid pools of desire.

'Oh yes,' she breathed. 'Please, Ricardo – please love me.'

It was what he had been waiting for. With a muffled cry, he buried his face in her hair and crushed her to him. Karen was aware of the hammering of his heart against her breasts, of the swift bloom of perspiration breaking through his pores. She could smell the heat of his skin, clean yet

10

musky, wholly masculine, and she felt her senses swim.

Gathering himself, Ricardo pulled back, gazing into her eyes for a long moment.

'So beautiful,' he murmured, his fingers tracing the outline of her features almost reverently, his eyes expressing wonder.

Karen *felt* beautiful, feminine in a way she had never felt before. She wanted to explore this feeling further, eager to experience all that it had to offer, but she wasn't sure what to do. Inwardly cursing her lack of experience, she could do nothing but wait passively for Ricardo to make the next move.

He moved away from her slightly so that he could run his eyes along the length of her body. Karen imagined that her skin tingled everywhere his gaze fell and she shivered. She felt vulnerable, exposed in spite of the token protection of her bikini. No man had never looked at her so openly before and she was relieved to read admiration in his eyes when he glanced at her.

He smiled as he ran the flat of his hand across her shoulder, smoothing and polishing the skin as he kneaded her arm. From her wrist, his fingertips fluttered across the silky planes of her stomach, making her muscles contract with the shock of the first touch.

Bending his head, he kissed a line along the valley between her breasts, nuzzling the indentation of her waist as his fingers described small, ticklish circles across her belly.

Karen was aware of a tightness in her stomach which extended downward into her most secret

11

places. Aware that the tender leaves of flesh had swollen and moistened, she fretted that he must be able to detect the perfume of her arousal, and she was embarrassed by it.

As if sensing her innocence, he raised his head and smiled gently at her.

'Relax, my sweet . . . trust how you feel.'

His voice was low and hypnotic, and he continued to talk to her as he led her gently along the path of fulfilment.

'Let me take this off . . .' he said, untying the strings which held her bikini top in place and peeling the tiny triangles of fabric away.

'Ahh, you have such lovely breasts, so round and full, making me want to hold and kiss them . . .'

He did just that, cupping one in his hand as if it were a rare and delicate object. As he drew her soft, rose-coloured nipple into his mouth Karen cried out, meshing her fingers in his hair and pressing him to her with an urgency which took her by surprise.

Nothing had prepared her for the exquisite sensation of his warm, gentle mouth suckling at her breast. She felt as if he was drawing the pleasure from deep within her, from a hidden, secret source she had never known existed.

When at last he drew back, she moaned in involuntary distress, the moan fading to a sigh as she realised he was only turning the attention to her other breast, not stopping entirely. Looking down at herself, she saw the now tumescent nipple pointing skyward, his saliva drying quickly in the sun, and she felt a sudden mule's kick of desire deep in the pit of her stomach. She had never dreamt it could be like this, that she could feel this good!

Emboldened, she moved her hips restlessly, eager for him to continue. Ricardo lifted his head and smiled at her, amused by her haste.

'Easy, my darling ... we've got all afternoon ...'

His lips captured hers, kissing her sweetly and then more deeply, his hands stroking her flesh more firmly, moulding her body to fit against his.

As his caresses became more urgent, more demanding, Karen felt a fresh rush of moisture seep from her, making the bikini wet with a heavier dampness than that of the sea water. Ricardo felt its warmth with the fingers he had pressed against her pubis, and judged her ready for more.

He watched her face as he unlaced the ribbon ties on either side of her hips.

'Do you trust me?' he asked, resting his warm hand palm-down against the gentle swell of her stomach.

'Yes,' she whispered, believing it. 'Please ...'

She wasn't sure as to what it was she was pleading for, she only knew she wanted him to go on, to show her how it could be between a man and a woman. They weren't boy and girl any longer – Karen knew she was growing up by the minute, that the girl who had climbed down to the beach would climb back up again as a woman.

'Please?' she murmured again, contracting her stomach muscles against his hand.

'Ssh ... lie still ...'

He slid down so that he was level with her hips.

Slowly, as if unveiling a work of art, he peeled the damp fabric away from her vulva, exposing her most private places to the kiss of the salty air and the warmth of his gaze.

Karen was aware of holding her breath, watching him to see what he would do next. Her labia felt as though they were buzzing silently, as if a permanent electrical charge was passing through them.

Levering herself up on to her elbows, she watched, wide-eyed, as he ran his forefinger lightly along the crease of her vulva, finishing at the apex. Deep inside her sex, her every nerve pulsed hopefully.

He opened her with his forefinger and thumb, gently parting her outer lips as if separating the petals of a flower. Her inner lips looked very pink, glistening with the honeyed secretions of her body.

Their eyes met and Ricardo smiled at her. Then, before she realised his intention, he dipped his head and ran the tip of his tongue swiftly, shockingly, along the cleft.

'Oh! Oh, no – don't!' she gasped, pulling his head away frantically.

'Why not? Don't you like it?'

He watched her closely, observing the tell-tale bloom on her skin, and smiled in satisfaction.

'I want to touch and taste you – all of you,' he told her, his fingers dabbling in the warm, wet places between her legs.

Karen tried to concentrate on what he was saying, but little ripples of pleasure were flowing outward from the centre of her sex, making it difficult to think, to rationalise anything.

14

Ricardo liked it, therefore it couldn't be wrong, she reasoned, as she pushed away her initial reticence and opened herself to him.

This time he buried his face in her sex with a groan, abandoning finesse as he lapped at the fount of her arousal. Karen gasped as she felt his tongue work its way into the opening to her body, while his fingers found the promontory of her clitoris and pressed against it.

'Oh, Ricardo!' she gasped, as he rubbed at the tender button of flesh, precipitating the sweetest, deepest climax she had ever experienced.

As the waves of ecstasy broke over her, Ricardo pressed his face against her sex, moving his lips across the convulsing flesh, and drinking in the thick honeydew which seeped from her. Karen writhed against the warm sand, alternately pulling away and grinding against him, wanting it to go on and on, to never stop.

When at last she was exhausted, he lifted his head and slid up her body so that he was lying alongside her. She could see her own bodily fluids glistening in the sun on his lips and chin and she swallowed, hard. She hadn't expected this. Had never dreamt that he would expect her to be so ... abandoned.

The colour of his eyes had deepened to that of dark chocolate, and they shone with a light she did not recognise. She felt the hardness of his erection pressing against the side of her thigh and realised that, far from being over, it had only just begun.

Seeing the uncertainty in her eyes, Ricardo drew her into the warm, welcoming circle of his arms

15

and kissed her. She could taste herself on his lips and tongue and she was momentarily ashamed, but once she realised that the flavour was fresh, almost sweet, she relaxed against him, kissing him back with a fervour that clearly surprised him.

'Are you all right?' he asked her when they broke apart.

'Of course.'

He nodded, satisfied by her response.

'Then I should like to make love to you.'

Looking down, Karen saw he had his penis in his hand, his thumb moving rhythmically across the smooth, circumcised tip, spreading the thin, clear moisture which leaked from its opening around the entire head. Her eyes widened as she realised how long and thick it was, doubtful that it would fit inside her. Surely it would hurt . . ?

'Ricardo – '

'Ssh!' He silenced her with another kiss. 'Bend up your knees and let them fall apart.'

Karen did as he asked, aware of his eyes on her exposed sex as he knelt between her legs.

'God, I want you,' he said.

His voice had taken on a curious, gravelly quality that Karen had never heard before. It affected her, making her juices flow so that she felt them running from her sex, down the crease between her buttocks and on to the warm sand.

Ricardo slipped his hands under her bottom and tilted her hips slightly, making access easier. She felt the moisture-slicked tip of his cock nudge at her opening, and then he thrust into her, all the way, with one firm, sure stroke.

16

A sharp, stinging pain seared her and she cried out in shock, her hands flying up to cling to him. Ricardo kept very still, not moving inside her, allowing her to get used to the sensation of fullness. He kissed her, so tenderly, and stroked her hair, murmuring endearments which calmed and soothed her. Slowly, slowly, Karen brought her breathing under control and allowed the desire to creep back.

Seeing that the initial pain had subsided, Ricardo murmured. 'All right?'

Staring into his eyes, Karen put her trust in him and nodded.

He began to move, merely rocking his hips back and forth to begin with, testing her reaction. Karen was aware of the discomfort sliding away into a slow, spreading warmth that intrigued her. She was ready when he began to thrust more deeply, holding on to his shoulders and moving her hips in time with his.

It was like a primitive, sacred dance, the rhythmic coming together and separating, the steadily increasing pace. Karen watched Ricardo's face, noting the tension in his jaw, the sheen of sweat across his top lip and his forehead. Under her fingers, she felt his muscles relax and contract, could feel the tension in him building to a crescendo. As he reached the peak, his entire body seemed to vibrate, in an exchange of energy that excited her beyond measure.

He came with a shout halfway between sub-mission and triumph, his ejaculation triggering a tremor of Karen's previous orgasm. Confident now that she knew what she was doing, she wrapped her legs around his waist and pulled him against her, reluctant to let him go.

Deep inside her she knew, without a doubt, that this was for always, forever, and that in Ricardo she had found the love of her life. Pulling his body yet tighter against hers, she rocked her hips so that her clitoris received the stimulation it needed to tip her into a second orgasm. This time it was even more intense than the first had been, her happiness changing her perception from the physical to the spiritual.

'I love you, Ricardo!' she cried, as they rolled together on the soft, warm sand.

'My darling – '

His voice was a cross between a groan and a sigh and she knew, without a doubt, that he felt the same way. Squeezing her pelvic floor muscles, she bound him to her, revelling in his shudder as she milked him dry.

'I love you, I love you, I love you,' she whispered fervently, placing dozens of tiny kisses across his face and on his neck.

Ricardo sought her mouth with his own and kissed her, binding her to him.

They came back down to earth slowly, wrapped in each other's arms. Karen felt as though they were contained in a large bubble, immured from everything but their love for each other. She had a sense of unreality which made her feel light-headed, and she continued to cling to Ricardo's shoulders as they became still.

'My darling – are you all right?'

Gradually, she became aware that Ricardo was stroking her hair, whispering soft words of endearment. His eyes, though, were troubled, and she rushed to reassure him.

'Of course! It was just that I never knew – I never dreamt it could be like that!'

He smiled at her, pleased with her response.

'I knew it would be good with us,' he told her confidently as they disengaged their bodies. 'We were made for each other.'

Karen liked the thought that they were meant to be together, and she smiled happily at him, barely aware of the unfamiliar, dull ache between her thighs.

'Come – let us swim again, yes?'

The lure of the warm water was strong and Karen allowed him to pull her to her feet. Her shyness about changing into her bikini in front of him seemed like the height of foolishness now, and they ran into the sea hand in hand, unselfconsciously naked.

The wash of the clear, warm salt water across her naked skin was exquisite. It cooled her, rinsing away all trace of their lovemaking, leaving her longing for more.

They made love again that afternoon, more fiercely this time, and with every stroke Karen's confidence grew. Cocooned in their own private world in the small bay, Ricardo showed her everything he knew about sex, so that by the time dusk began to fall, Karen felt as if all the secrets of the universe were within her grasp.

Reluctantly, they climbed the steep cliff path,

carrying their wet towels. Once they reached the bike, both turned, as if by an unspoken agreement, to look out across the darkened bay.

It was a clear, starry night and the full moon hung low in the sky, so that the grey-black sea was filmed with silver. The seabirds were silent now, their cries replaced by the incessant hum of insects calling to each other on the warm night air.

Gazing across the bay, Karen felt as perfect as the scene before her. She leant happily into Ricardo's body as he slipped his arms around her waist and rested his chin on the top of her head. She felt tired in a way she had never felt before: her body was sore and heavy, but not unpleasantly so, and she imagined she could still feel the imprint of his slender, clever cock deep inside her.

'Beautiful, isn't it?' he murmured after a few moments of silent harmony.

'Breathtaking. I'll remember this day, this moment, all my life,' she whispered solemnly. 'I've never felt as happy as this . . .'

Turning her around in his arms, Ricardo kissed her lingeringly. 'This is just the beginning,' he promised her, his hands moving softly over her body.

And she had believed him. With all her heart and mind, she had believed him . . .

Chapter One

Karen sat across from the manager of the travel agency where she worked and waited patiently for him to stop fiddling with the paraphernalia littering his desk. He seemed nervous, his pale blue eyes never quite meeting hers when he looked at her. From the way he was holding himself, rigid with tension, she guessed that beneath the plain, utilitarian office desk, he had an erection of monstrous proportions, and she deliberately crossed her legs, giving him a tantalising glimpse of smooth, tanned thigh.

Aaron's eyes flickered from her legs to her face before looking quickly away again. A slight flush stained his skin along his cheekbones and Karen smiled to herself. She loved this: the knowledge that she could turn a man on at will, at any time of the night or day. True, Aaron had taken time to allow himself to be drawn into her seductive web, but the victory was all the sweeter for that. It always was.

'I – er – we have a problem,' he told her now, struggling manfully to maintain control in the business environment.

'Oh?' Karen said coolly when he did not elaborate. She had been waiting for this, for him to find some excuse to remove her from his immediate orbit, no doubt in the pitiful hope that he would be able to forget his dark cravings. 'Something to do with my work?'

'Of course not! No, it's nothing to do with you personally, Karen. You know that your skills are valued very highly . . .' He trailed off as he recognised the unintentional *double entendre*.

Karen smiled ingenuously at him. 'Then what kind of problem is it that you – *we* have?' she asked, sweetly.

'Wingspan have lost another rep and they've asked us to find a replacement. Now that the season is underway you know it will be difficult to fill the post, especially at such short notice.'

'I see. Where is this vacancy?' Karen asked, her interest piqued.

'In the Med. I wondered if you . . .?' Aaron trailed off again, embarrassed as he realised that, however he put it, Karen would interpret this suggestion as a bid to send her away.

She laughed, as if reading his thoughts.

'Dear Aaron – did you think you could escape so easily? After all, who's going to give you what you need if I go away? Do you think the lovely Serena would oblige?'

Aaron flushed at the mention of his fiancée, and glared at Karen with something close to dislike. Good, she congratulated herself, smugly. It was always so much better when they told themselves that they disliked her. It made the way they kept coming back for more all the more satisfying.

Gazing out of the window at the rainswept inner London streets, she thought wistfully for a moment of the Mediterranean sky. It had been ten years since she had last been there, in her first post as a travel rep. Her face hardened. Though she wasn't particularly ambitious in her career, personally she'd come a long way since then.

'Does that mean that you're not interested in going?'

Karen shifted her attention as lackadaisically as possible and gave him a smile. 'Tell me more – it might be a change.'

Trying unsuccessfully to hide the pang her casual attitude gave him, Aaron picked up a file and opened it.

'It's in Tierra del Sol . . .'

His voice droned on as Karen absorbed the shock. *Tierra del Sol*. Even now, after all these years, the mere sound of the name made all her hard-won confidence drain away. What were the chances of this happening? Of all places, the one resort to which she had sworn never to return . . .

'I know it,' she interrupted Aaron, standing up so abruptly that he looked up at her in surprise.

'Well – what do you think?'

Karen paused on her way to the door. Could she

23

bear to go back? After all, she wasn't a naive eighteen-year-old on her first job now.

'I'll think about it,' she said non-committally. 'Give me the file.'

Aaron rose and handed it to her, keeping the desk between them as if for protection. Noticing the action, Karen felt the strength flow back into her. She was a different person now: no one could ever hurt her as she had been hurt that summer. No one would even dare to try.

'Karen?' he said as she turned away.

'Yes?'

'There is another reason why I'd like you to handle this.'

Karen turned back, giving him her full attention. If she hadn't known him better, she would have described his expression as shifty. She smiled to herself at the incongruity of the word.

'As you know, I've been looking at ways to – to branch out from the travel agency . . .'

Karen felt a small twinge of sympathy for him as she realised how much he felt in his father's shadow.

'And?' she prompted, compassion quickly sliding into impatience as he prevaricated.

'Tierra del Sol looks set to be *the* holiday mecca over the next couple of years. I'd like you to have a look around; see if you can find a suitable location for a hotel.'

Karen raised her eyebrows. 'So you have sufficient capital for a venture like that?' she asked.

Aaron's brows drew together in a frown. 'That's

my concern,' he told her stiffly. 'It goes without saying that your role would be amply rewarded.'

Not bothering to hide her amusement at his pomposity, Karen nodded.

'Quite. I'll think about it, Aaron.'

'Wait – there's . . . something else.'

Karen turned and looked at him expectantly.

'Yes?'

Aaron cleared his throat and stared at her. He was a handsome guy, Karen thought dispassionately, if you liked your men symmetrical. His hair was thick and dark blond and the faint lines which ran from the sides of his nose to the corners of his mouth would deepen over the years to form attractive grooves. As the son of the owner of the travel company, he had the air of assurance that only a top-notch education could bestow, a polished edge which helped to smooth his way through life.

To look at him, any woman would think he was so together, so self-controlled. Karen knew differently and it changed the way she saw him.

'Well?' she said, impatiently now.

'Tonight. Is it still on for tonight?' He almost spat out the words, as if he had to say them even though it cost him a great deal.

Karen allowed her lips to curl into a sneer and Aaron trembled with suppressed pleasure.

'You're forgetting, I have a report to read,' she told him, waving the folder.

'You can read it tomorrow.'

'It's my day off tomorrow.'

'Please – '

'Make it tomorrow night. Come around at eight.'

Without waiting for a reply, Karen marched out of his office.

'What did he want?' Olivia asked her as she sat down at a terminal.

Karen smiled gently at her, hearing the note of envy in her voice. Olivia had been heartbroken when Aaron had become engaged to Serena and she still wore her heart on her sleeve. If only she knew what a disappointment he would be to her!

'Apparently there's a chance I could be spending the summer in the Med.' She grinned at Olivia's blatant envy.

'You lucky cow!' said the girl good-naturedly. 'How come you get all the luck?'

'Previous experience,' Karen said, adding silently *and getting under the boss's skin*. 'Actually, I'm not sure whether to go.'

'What? You must be mad to even think twice! Why, Karen?' she asked curiously, as she saw her friend's expression. 'Is there some reason *why* you wouldn't want to go?'

Karen, who had been staring, unseeingly, at the monitor in front of her, turned a small, self-deprecating smile on the other girl.

'I'm probably being daft. It's just that I knew someone there once.'

'Someone who hurt you?' Olivia said perceptively.

Karen had a brief flash of soulful dark eyes, and of olive skin sliding slowly across hers, and she shivered. She didn't want to think about it, not even now.

'Yes,' she replied simply, 'I – '

At that moment, a customer came into the shop, closely followed by several noisy children. Olivia shot Karen a rueful glance and turned her attention to the job.

Thrusting aside the memory of firm, warm lips pressing tenderly against the soft skin of her inner thighs, Karen resolutely shoved the folder into her desk drawer and went back to work.

The bars and clubs along the main streets of Leventos, the tourist capital of Tierra del Sol, began to fill slowly. It had been a glorious day and the hordes of young holidaymakers who made up the majority of the resort's clientele had been sleeping off the previous night's excesses on the beach.

Ricardo Baddeiras stood outside the Bar del Amore and shaded his eyes from the sun. A group of girls was walking with self-conscious bravado along the street, pretending to be unaware of the lascivious glances they were attracting. Ricardo narrowed his eyes, admiring the bare legs which emerged from their shorts and mini skirts. He could tell from the colour of their skin that these girls were coming to the end of their holiday. Lily-white to begin with, most of the fair-skinned English progressed through a delicate pink to caramel by the end of the first week, though a few unfortunates, the more careless, turned a bright, painful shade of lobster.

The tallest of the five girls, who were now drawing level with his bar, looked vaguely familiar, though, with her long, dark hair and slender figure she was of a physical type that Ricardo found appealing, so it was hardly surprising that his eyes were drawn to her. He smiled as she reached him.

'Hello Ric,' she said, her voice soft and breathy.

It was a voice that Ricardo recognised. Some nights before it had gasped obscenities at him in the height of passion; words which had shocked him, coming from so soft a mouth. He smiled in the way he knew all the girls liked, frantically searching his memory banks for her name. It was no good: the season had only just got underway and already she was lost in the crowd.

'Hello darling,' he greeted her, kissing her on both cheeks whilst holding her away from him. She smelt of sun oil and cheap perfume, and the feel of her skin beneath his lips was unfamiliar.

'I'm going home tomorrow.'

Though her tone was light and chatty, her eyes searched his, as if she was hoping he might show some genuine regret. Ricardo carefully kept his expression neutral and uninvolved as he wished her well, trying not to notice the way her face fell at his formality.

'I hope you enjoyed your holiday?' he enquired politely of the group in general.

Most of them giggled engagingly, and after a few minutes they moved on. Ricardo went inside to escape the tall brunette's wistful glances over her shoulder. It made him feel like one of his bar boys – a stud. The thought didn't give him any pleasure. In truth he knew he would prefer to sleep only with girls whose names he knew, and beside whom he might wish to wake in the morning. So many meaningless flings reduced the act of making love to a mere physical release, like sneezing.

When had he tired of the chase? Ricardo sighed, conscious of a heaviness in his heart that never quite seemed to leave him. There had been a girl once, an English girl. Between them it had been the closest he had ever come to perfection, before or since. But he had been too young to appreciate what he had found, and by the time his head had caught up with his heart she had gone, without a word of farewell.

Ricardo shook his head, angry with himself for allowing the memories to haunt him. These English girls! They were all the same. Ricardo had spent some time in England as a student, so he knew that the image they presented on holiday was not a representation of typical English womanhood. Back in England they had lives and jobs and serious pursuits to take their minds off sex. But once they arrived in Tierra del Sol – God Almighty! It was as if they shed all their inhibitions with their warm clothing. All they wanted was sun, sea and sex, and not necessarily in that order.

Which was why, Ricardo reminded himself as he eyed the young men milling around in his bar, he employed these youthful studs to lure the female tourists into the place – and then give them what they wanted.

'There's a guy out back who wants to see you, Ric.'

Ricardo raised his eyebrows quizzically at the young man who had spoken. Darren had returned for his fifth season at the bar and as such was afforded a kind of seniority.

'Who?' he asked him.

'From the tour company.' Darren made a face at him before turning his attention to taking the barstools down from the tables.

Of course. Ricardo sighed as he made his way to the back office. He might have guessed there would be repercussions after last week's incident. Yet another young woman who had mistaken lust for love had complained to her tour guide when one of his staff had disillusioned her. The boy could have been more tactful, it was true, but Ricardo failed to see why the tour guide should have been so shocked by what she had found going on at the bar. He had heard afterwards that she had decided that the job wasn't for her after all and had packed her bags and fled back home.

Ricardo could see the travel company rep through the glass window of his office door, sweating in a shiny grey suit, and his heart sank. Maria was with him, smiling and charming him, but Ricardo knew that there was nothing his sister could do to avert the row that was brewing.

Maybe he was getting old, losing his touch. Whatever, of one thing he was sure – this job wasn't fun any more.

Karen was waiting for Aaron in the hallway of her house when he arrived, on the dot of eight. As soon as he saw the short, shiny black PVC mac and matching ankle boots she was wearing, he began to tremble visibly. Standing, legs akimbo, her hands planted firmly on her hips, Karen eyed him with contempt.

'So – here you are, crawling in for your weekly dose of humiliation! And to think, you really believe that you'll get by without me once I've gone to Tierra del Sol.'

'You've decided to go?' There was a leap of hope in Aaron's eyes which was quickly doused by anguish. Poor Aaron – he really didn't know what he wanted.

'I might.'

Ever since Karen had read Ricardo Baddeiras' name in the Wingspan report she had been imagining how it might be if she went back. She was a woman now, not a silly, lovestruck girl. More than a match for Señor Baddeiras. The thought had aroused her, made her feel restless and demanding. She smiled at Aaron, glad now that he was here. In her mind's eye, she superimposed Ricardo's dark and haughty face on to Aaron's bland features and a pulse began to beat between her legs. If she could only get her hands on him . . .

'Did you bring it?'

Aaron, who had been staring at her, his eyes wide, like a rabbit caught in the headlights of an oncoming car, blinked and reached into his briefcase.

'Yes, Karen, I brought the short-handled whip this time. I hope that's all right?'

He didn't move as she leant forward and took the whip from his lifeless hand, though his eyes followed the movement as though he were hypnotised.

31

Karen did not reply. Holding the handle in one hand, she caressed it lovingly with the other, her fingertips tracing the intricate pattern carved into the soft, pliable leather. It gave her a thrill just to touch it. If it hadn't been for Ricardo, she might never had discovered this singular pleasure, she reflected, spinning out the tension. Without her anger and her hurt at his betrayal of her, she might never have found the drive to dominate and punish, and might never have experienced the thrill she derived from doing so to such devastating effect.

Aaron watched her, his tongue moving along his upper lip to catch the droplets of sweat which had formed on the surface. Glancing down, she saw the fabric of his suit pants straining against the fly fastening. She smiled.

'Well, well, well! What have we here?' she hissed, trailing the tip of the whip lightly across the front of his trousers.

Aaron shuddered, staring at her with an expression that caused a dark thrill in the pit of her belly. She knew that he was desperately trying to fight his urges. They went through this ritual every time, even though both of them knew she would win in the end. She always did, for she was the one with the whip – the one with the power.

Aaron liked to think he was a man's man, an all-drinking, all-smoking, womanising braggart. The games to which she had introduced him undermined everything he thought he knew about himself, yet he always came back for more.

Looking at him now, so handsome and urbane,

oozing charm and success, Karen wondered what gremlin he possessed, what recalcitrant gene it was that gave him such dark desires.

'Shall we go up to the bedroom?' he asked, his voice husky with need.

'I think not – the hallway will suffice.' Karen smiled at his look of horror. He was such a conventional little soul at heart. 'Take them off,' she said curtly, indicating his trousers.

Aaron stared at her and for a moment she thought he would turn around and leave. The conflict she could read in his eyes excited her, making her innermost flesh pulse and swell as she watched him battle with himself. When he gave in and unzipped his trousers, Karen thought she would come there and then.

'Kneel down and lie across the phone table,' she told him, once he stood naked but for his shirt and tie in front of her.

The surge of power which rushed through her veins as he obeyed her made Karen feel exultant. Aaron's buttocks looked very white against the red velour of the telephone seat. Leaning forward, Karen ran her fingertip from his waist to the bottom of his spine, noting how his buttocks clenched as she reached the beginning of his cleft. She smiled to herself.

'This will never do,' she said softly, 'not if you want me to let you come. And you do want me to let you come, don't you Aaron?' she crooned.

'Bitch!' Aaron said between his teeth, though his voice quivered, betraying his excitement.

Karen laughed.

'Oh, you'll have to pay for that! Spread your knees apart!'

Aaron obeyed, reluctantly, and Karen walked around him, making a show of looking at him.

'Hmm. Better. Now let me see . . . what next? A little . . . *anticipation*, I think – it always helps to add a little spice to things.'

Aaron gazed up at her, not understanding. Possessed of a sudden, mischievous urge, Karen reached into the neckline of her mac and lifted out one full, rose-tipped breast. Aaron's eyes widened, his breathing becoming shallow as she rolled the nipple between her forefinger and thumb, teasing it to hardness.

As the invisible thread connecting her nipple and womb tugged at her nerve endings, Karen allowed herself a moment's self-indulgence. Closing her eyes, she tipped her head back slightly, allowing her lips to part in a sigh of pure narcissistic pleasure.

She knew her own body so well: every tender spot, each supercharged nerveline. If she so wished, she could bring herself to orgasm within minutes, simply by manipulating her nipples. Sensing that her attention had drifted away from him, Aaron made a small noise of protest, forcing her back to reality.

Opening her eyes, she looked coldly at him. His pupils grew larger, almost obscuring the iris as he waited for her next move. Slowly, Karen trailed the tails of the short-handled whip across the contours of her exposed breast. The thin leather felt cool and soft, and she sighed.

Holding Aaron's eye, she tucked her breast back inside the PVC mac and walked slowly towards him. He was waiting for her like a dog hoping to be taken for a walk, placing the responsibility for his pleasure as well as her own firmly in her hands. Karen felt a sharp stab of contempt which made her lip curl.

Aaron shuddered as if the gesture had physically touched him.

'What am I to do with you?' she murmured, half to herself.

Aaron winced as she flicked her wrist and the tails of the whip slapped lightly against his right buttock. He sucked in his breath as the blood rose to the surface of his skin. Flicking the other buttock, she waited until it had turned the same blush pink as its twin before delivering two more, slightly harder blows, in quick succession.

Aaron was breathing heavily now and Karen was aware that her own chest was rising and falling as her arousal grew. The skin of his buttocks glowed a deep, even pink. Karen paused for long enough to lean over him and place a cool hand on his burning skin. Aaron groaned, though whether in pain or with pleasure it was difficult to tell.

Karen let her hand slip softly into the heated crease between his buttocks. Aaron automatically clenched his muscles, momentarily trapping her hand between them as he denied himself the pleasure of her touch.

Slapping him lightly with the palm of her other hand, Karen felt him let go, the flesh of his bottom slackening and softening, allowing his buttocks to

35

fall apart. Sliding one finger downward, she skipped lightly over the puckered whorl of his anus and scraped her long fingernails gently across the back of his balls.

The effect was electrifying. With a muttered curse, Aaron reared up on his knees and ran his hand up and down his shaft, quickly, several times. Within seconds he came, spattering his seed across the parquet floor in a series of violent spurts. Karen was furious, as much with herself for precipitating the crisis too soon as with him for his lack of control.

'How dare you!' she breathed icily.

Aaron turned to her, his eyes still glazed, his rapidly deflating prick still held in his hand. He flinched as she raised the whip and brought it down across his shoulders, yet the expression which passed across his eyes was one of unmistakable excitement. Karen pushed him down on to his back and straddled him, one knee on each shoulder.

He didn't need any instruction as she lowered herself on to his face. She was naked under the short mac and Aaron's lips and tongue moved hungrily over her swollen labia, parting them and exposing her burgeoning clitoris. Karen arched her back, rolling her nipples against her own palms as Aaron began a rhythmic licking and sucking at her flesh. She rode him, sliding her sex backwards and forwards across his face as the sensations began to build and she grew more frantic.

The man underneath her ceased to exist as a living, breathing person: to Karen he was merely a means to an end, an arrangement of lips and tongue and teeth, brought into play purely for her pleasure. She used him as she might have used a dildo, relentlessly and without a thought for his needs, and hardly any for his comfort.

As her climax broke, she ground her pelvis against his nose and mouth, so that by the time she climbed off him he was gasping for air and spluttering. Breathing heavily herself, Karen climbed off him and stood up. She gazed down at him for a moment as he lay, supine on the floor, looking up at her.

His cock had rallied after its earlier exertions, and was standing straight as a sentinel, rearing up hopefully from his groin. Allowing her upper lip to rise in a sneer, Karen nudged it with the toe of her boot.

'Put it away, Aaron – the sight of you sickens me.'

As always, her display of contempt made him whimper with longing, but this time her revulsion was not all feigned. Suddenly, she felt unutterably weary. What was she doing here? What the hell was it all about?

Straightening her mac, Karen calmly picked up Aaron's trousers from the floor. When she could trust herself to speak, she passed them to him.

'Time to go, Aaron,' she said firmly.

Scrambling inelegantly to his feet, he looked at her with a mixture of resentment and something else; an admiration that sent a dark thrill through her, reaffirming her resolve.

'Just like that?' he asked her, when he found his

voice. 'You're just going to use me, then throw me out? You haven't even let me past the hallway!'

Karen smiled serenely. 'Close the door behind you on your way out,' she said dismissively, turning her back on him and heading for the bathroom. 'Oh, and by the way – ' she turned as he reached the door and smiled sweetly at him ' – I won't be in on Monday. I've decided that I will take the job in Tierra del Sol.'

Turning her back on Aaron's crestfallen expression, Karen thought about what would happen when she met Ricardo again. She heard the door click shut behind Aaron, but she had already forgotten about him as she turned her thoughts to the sweet contemplation of revenge.

Chapter Two

*O*nce she had made the decision to go to Tierra del Sol, things moved fast. Deciding she would let her flat on a short-term lease, Karen packed up her belongings and put the matter in the hands of an estate agent friend. Paula would make sure that the place was well looked after while she was away, and would make her own spare room available if Karen decided to leave Tierra del Sol earlier than planned.

Not that there was any logical reason why she should come home prematurely, she told herself irritably as she packed. It wasn't as if she expected to be in the least bit affected by seeing Ricardo again.

In the long term, it made her feel more in control once she had covered all eventualities, and she was relatively calm the day before her departure.

'You're all packed, I presume?'

She looked up to find Aaron hovering around her desk, looking uncomfortable.

'Of course. Did you think I might change my mind?' she asked, unable to resist teasing him.

Aaron's eyes darkened and he seemed to be unable to hold her eye.

'I'll be in touch ... about the other business. Have a good trip.' Turning abruptly, he retreated to his office, leaving Karen to deal with Olivia's blatant stare.

'What was all that about?' the younger girl asked, as soon as the door had closed behind him.

Karen shrugged. 'I guess he's going to miss me,' she said flippantly.

'Hmm, I suppose he is.'

Karen looked up in surprise as she heard the thoughtful note in Olivia's voice.

'Hey! I was only kidding!' she protested mildly.

'Were you? Come on, Karen – it's an open secret about you and Aaron. Let's face it, you're a far better catch than that milksop of a fiancée of his!'

Karen laughed at the old-fashioned turn of phrase and shook her head.

'They probably suit each other. Listen, the only person I'm going to miss from this office is you, so take care of yourself and keep in touch, okay?'

The two women smiled at each other, both valuing the friendship they had built up over the months.

Later, on leaving the office, Karen was handed a full report written by the travel rep who had resigned so hurriedly. The initial report had outlined no more than the bare bones of her complaint, but in this account she had, to some extent, put professionalism aside and written from the heart.

Waiting until she had enjoyed a long soak in a warm bath, Karen took it into the bedroom to read. The girl, Deirdre, had a gift for making her words come off the page and Karen was easily able to imagine the scenes she described.

I enjoy my work as a Wingspan representative, Karen read, *the people I meet are, on the whole, lovely people. But I have never encountered such debauchery as that which takes place in certain bars in Tierra del Sol.*

The type of holidays offered by Wingspan generally appeal to a younger age group than average, particularly to young women. The hotels and apartments I cover are largely occupied by all-female parties. Most of the girls have come for sun, sea, and, in some cases, sex. They do not come to be abused and humiliated by certain predatory 'studs' who work in the bars and clubs on the island.

I have been unhappy with the general atmosphere and attitudes here for some time, but it was one incident in particular that, for me, tipped the balance. This concerned a young tourist who fancied herself to be genuinely in love with one of these bar boys. By the second week of her holiday, she was making plans to move permanently to the resort on the basis of promises made to her by this man.

When she discovered him with another tourist, barely an hour after she herself had left his bed, she was, naturally, upset. She became all the more so when, having retreated in distress to the quarters shared by the bar boys, she found her name had been added to a large chart pinned to the wall. The chart, which I have seen myself, is designed to grade the women sexually on a points system ranging from 'pigs' to 'juicy peaches'. Full details of their attributes, plus a list of what they were and were not willing to do in bed were displayed clearly for all to see.

Worse still, the girl discovered that photographs had been taken of her with her boyfriend, some of which had been enlarged and pasted to the walls. A pile of unmarked video tapes in the corner of the room led her to suspect that their trysts had also been filmed.

I admit that she was naive, but her distress when she discovered that she had been used was so pitiful, I decided to confront the owner of the bar in order to stop such a thing happening again. Unfortunately, Senor Baddeiras was less than sympathetic to the girl's plight and, indeed, seemed to find my own indignation somewhat amusing.

'I left when he suggested that my true complaint was that I should not, myself, score too highly on the bar boys' 'shagometer'.

Karen closed the report, unable to read any more. A young tourist had fancied herself to be genuinely in love . . . It was too painful to consider. That Ricardo should have sunk so low filled her with a mixture of fury and sorrow. It sounded as though the men on Tierra del Sol had been given free rein for far too long.

As far as Karen was concerned, there was nothing wrong with casual sex, so long as both parties respected one another – even if that respect only extended to making each other aware of the exact basis of the relationship. In Karen's book, if the girl had been aware of being filmed and photographed, that would have been fine. What was unacceptable to her was the way in which the girl had been duped, and her feelings taken to be of no account, even after the event.

The travel rep was right, she had been used. Much the same as Karen had been used, all those years ago.

Closing her eyes, she allowed the image of Ricardo's face to swim into her mind. Time had not blurred the picture; it was as sharp and clear as if she had seen him only yesterday – No! she wouldn't think of it now. There was still too much to do, so many plans to make.

With a huge effort of will, Karen pushed the thought of Ricardo and his bar boys to the back of her mind and turned her attention to the file Aaron had given her on his proposed project. Looking for suitable land was going to distract her from the more mundane aspects of her job as a stand-in travel rep for Wingspan. Maybe it would also serve to distract her from the memory of Ricardo's lips on hers.

'Oh, for God's sake!' Karen said aloud as she jumped up from the chair.

She was tired, bone-weary, and she went back into the bedroom, pulling the covers up around her neck and closing her eyes with hopeless resolution. It irritated her to remember herself as she had been ten years before. She had been so trusting, so naive.

No one would ever dare to try to hurt her

now. Since that first, hopelessly romantic sexual awakening with Ricardo, Karen had taken her pleasures when and where she wanted to, keeping her heart firmly under control.

As far as she was concerned, men were only good for one thing. For the finer things of life, like friendship, compassion and fun, she relied upon her numerous female friends. She would have preferred to have been born a lesbian, if the truth be known, but her one foray in that direction had been little short of a disaster, leaving her cold.

Men were, therefore, a necessary evil in her life, if she was to continue to be sexually fulfilled. Thank God she'd stumbled upon her natural skill to dominate and control them!

Briefly, she wondered what Ricardo would think of her now? Her mouth set in a hard line – she'd love to show *him* what she'd learned . . .

A sharp image of him kneeling before her, his hands bound behind him, his back bent in supplication, sent a rush of pure lust through to her groin. Sitting up with a groan, she realised that trying to sleep was useless. Lying back on her bed, she hitched the silk chemise she was wearing up around her waist and curled her fingers into the hot, moist flesh of her vulva.

It would give her an enormous amount of pleasure to have Ricardo at her mercy. She would stripe the smooth, golden skin she remembered, leaving him with a badge of shame that he would carry, deep in his heart, long after the actual physical marks had faded.

Fresh moisture coated Karen's circling fingers as

she imagined the satisfaction of his surrender. She would break him down, minute by minute, hour by hour, until he no longer knew who he was, or what he wanted. But *she* would know, she knew they all wanted the same thing in the end. He would be no different, nothing special.

She knew now how to make a man want her so much he would crawl naked on his hands and knees for the privilege of kissing her boots, suffer any indignity for the honour of touching his lips against her flesh. If she wanted to be licked, or sucked, or even fucked, Karen knew exactly which buttons to press, and when. And she knew how to bind a man to her, body and soul, so that his sexual responses would never again belong to him alone.

She came, swiftly and sharply, pressing her fingertips against the pulsing bud of her clitoris until every last vestige of sensation had passed. Then she pulled the covers up over her ears, and quickly fell asleep.

In her dreams she travelled back in time to become, once more, her eighteen-year-old self, preoccupied with her lover and the bliss they shared. Her job had become an irritation in those long, lazy weeks of the summer, nothing more than a barrier between her and the time she wanted to share with Ricardo.

After that first time, she couldn't get enough of him: she wanted to make love all day every day, to possess him totally, utterly, beyond all measure of doubt. Perhaps, deep down, despite her inexperience, she knew he was never really hers, but that he had merely lent himself to her for a while.

Ricardo's enthusiasm never waned, though Karen noticed that, occasionally, he wasn't as ardent as usual. This she put down to tiredness: Ricardo's father was terminally ill and fading rapidly. Understandably, father and son spent a great deal of time together, not least because he owned a bar on the tourist strip of Leventos in Tierra del Sol and Ricardo was being groomed to take it over.

It was a dingy place, underdeveloped and tawdry, and Karen hated going there. It was frequented mostly by local men and elderly lechers on holiday, attracted by the pretty waitresses and indifferent exotic dancers who performed twice nightly.

Ricardo had great plans for the place, though, and Karen did her best to encourage him. When his father died, he told her, he would have the finance to revamp the place and make it more attractive to the younger crowd who were beginning to flock to Tierra del Sol on their package deals.

'You'll have to get rid of this sort of thing,' Karen had said, nodding towards the stripper on the podium.

The woman had been bottle-blonde with a sad-looking face, accentuated now by an expression of utter boredom. Dressed in nothing but a pair of spangled panties, she gyrated suggestively against a pole. It should have been sexy, but instead it was about the least erotic spectacle Karen had ever witnessed. She caught Ricardo's eye and they both burst out laughing.

'I'll bring in men to tempt the women,' he told her, reaching forward to touch her cheek. He was always touching her, kissing her, as if he wanted to keep making sure she was real. 'What do you think? Would you want to go to a bar where a dozen men are trained to make you feel like a queen?'

'One will do for me,' she had told him softly, leaning forward to touch her lips to his.

It was later that same evening, after Ricardo had taken her back to her lodgings on his scooter, that she realised she had left her bag at the bar. Normally, she wouldn't have bothered to go back for it, knowing that she would be seeing Ricardo the following day. This time, though, they had agreed that he would sit with his father all day, and they had made no plans to meet until the day after. Karen needed that bag; it had the list of new arrivals due the following morning inside it, so she decided to cycle the short distance back to the bar.

Pedro, the elderly barman, looked surprised to see her.

'I was just locking up, *Señorita*,' he said, opening the door for her.

'It's all right, Pedro, I've just come back for my bag. Has Ricardo left it behind the bar for me?'

Pedro shrugged his old shoulders expressively.

'Well, where is Ricardo? Is he upstairs?'

Ricardo often stayed at the bar when he had worked later: there was a small apartment upstairs which housed the basic utilities, and Karen had often spent a few hours there, their passion lending it a glamour it most definitely did not possess.

Without bothering to wait for Pedro's reply,

47

Karen took the stairs two at a time, happy to have a legitimate excuse to prolong her time with Ricardo. Maybe she could stay the night . . .

She stopped dead in her tracks as she burst into the bedroom, hoping to surprise him. She had surprised him all right, she realised bitterly, as she recognised the bottle-blonde stripper bouncing up and down on top of him. The woman's breasts were squashed against Ricardo's palms and he was arching his back, his neck muscles tense and taut as he strove towards orgasm.

As Karen burst through the door, the woman turned her head slowly, her expression blank. Neither woman had to say anything: that small movement alone alerted Ricardo.

'Karen – '

She staggered to the bathroom to be sick. The image of the naked woman sitting astride Ricardo, his cock buried deep within her body, was seared into her mind. But worse, much worse, had been the look on Ricardo's face.

Karen knew that look – knew it and had thought it was reserved for her alone. The glazed, ecstatic expression that always came over his face in the seconds before he came, the look she had mistaken for love.

She whirled around as he appeared in the doorway to the bathroom, a towel tied around his waist.

'Karen? Darling – '

'Don't touch me!' she cried, as he reached for her.

She could smell the stripper's cheap perfume clinging to his skin, together with the unmistakable odour of sex.

'How could you?' she cried, anguish pushing pride away. 'And with that . . . woman?'

'Karen – '

'Shut up! I don't want to listen to you, I never want to listen to you again! How could you have been turned on by the performance she gave tonight? All the time we were sitting together, you were watching her, knowing you could screw her when I went home – ' she shuddered at the thought, overcome with shame ' – I hate you – hate you!'

She had pushed past him and run blindly down the stairs, past the startled Pedro and out into the night.

It was impossible to stay on the island once her dreams of love with Ricardo had been shattered. It was an easy matter to book herself on the next flight home.

As the plane took off, Karen refused to look back. Ricardo's betrayal was like an open wound, aching and festering. *Never again*, she vowed. And she knew that one day she would return to Tierra del Sol and make him pay . . . and pay . . .

'Fasten your safety belts, please, we will shortly be landing. Welcome to Tierra del Sol.'

Karen looked out of the window at her first glimpse of the island since her bitter departure, ten years before. Its terracotta land looked hot and arid, though it was surrounded by a sea so blue it sparkled like a sapphire-encrusted cloak in the sun.

As the plane descended, she saw the golden beaches fringing the coast and the memories assaulted her without mercy: Ricardo laughing, squinting at her in the sunshine; Ricardo running with her in his arms to dump her, squealing, into the water; Ricardo leaning over her on the soft, warm sand, his eyes lambent, filled with love . . .

Stop! Karen wrenched her eyes away from the window, angry with herself for allowing the good times to haunt her. If she was to see Ricardo again and face him with any degree of equanimity, she had to keep his betrayal in focus, to remember that behind his handsome face, there was nothing but lies and emptiness.

'Are you all right, Miss?'

Karen started as the young air steward leant over her, speaking softly. Gazing up at him, she saw he was a soft-skinned youth, with the kind of complexion which would redden with embarrassing frequency. It was flushing now as he looked into Karen's eyes and saw the wealth of sensual promise in their depths. She felt a sudden, unexpected rush of desire as she read his reaction in his pale grey eyes.

'C – can I get you anything?' he said, his voice rising slightly.

Karen smiled slowly.

'I need a slight . . . adjustment to my clothing,' she purred. Reaching up, she ran her fingernail lightly down his shirt front, circling the smooth, flat disc of one nipple before scratching gently at it with her long, red-painted fingernail.

The steward gulped audibly, his pupils dilating with a mixture of excitement and alarm.

'Perhaps you could come to the toilets with me

50

and help?' Karen said huskily, allowing her lips to form a perfect Bardot pout.

Straightening, he glanced nervously up and down the aisle.

'We'll be landing in fifteen minutes – '

'It won't take that long.'

'Perhaps a female stewardness . . .?'

Karen fixed him with a compelling gaze.

'You'll do just fine . . . Justin,' she said, cocking her head to one side to read his name badge.

Justin swallowed convulsively and, with a brief jerk of his head which Karen took to be a nod, he made his way to the toilet cubicle.

No one challenged Karen as she stood up and followed him. The FASTEN YOUR SEATBELT signs were illuminated and most passengers obeyed at once, but Karen had other, more pressing needs than safety to consider.

Justin squeezed up against the toilet bowl as Karen eased herself into the cubicle. His tension was like a tangible thing, hanging in the small space, making it claustrophobic. Karen smiled slowly, her eyes passing knowingly over the tell-tale bulge in the front of his black, standard-issue trousers.

'Sit down,' she said, her eyes indicating the closed toilet seat.

The steward did as he was told. His eyes were huge as he gazed up at her and she could feel him trembling, sense his instinctive fear of her. It made her feel powerful, feminine in a way that had become addictive.

Holding his eye, she unbuttoned her blouse and

51

freed one of her breasts, its nipple already flushing pink and semi-erect, from its lacy confinement.

'Suck this,' she instructed him, leaning over slightly to make his task easier.

His lips were smooth and hot as they closed over the soft areola. Karen drew in her breath as she felt the echo of the pull of his lips on her teat deep in her womb. Her inner muscles contracted, turning her pleasure to an urgent, liquid heat. Slipping her hand down the front of her loose trousers, she circled the bud of her clitoris through her lace panties.

The scent of her arousal was strong in the confined space: she could smell it and knew that the boy could, too. His erection had grown, tenting the front of his trousers, but Karen wasn't interested in his needs, only in the steadily beating pulse of her own sex.

'Harder,' she whispered urgently, as her fingers worked their way under the elastic of her knickers to touch the slippery flesh. 'Suck harder, damn you!'

Justin obliged, making small, incoherent noises in the back of his throat as her nipple swelled and filled his mouth. Karen knew it was difficult for him to breathe as her breast squashed against his nose and mouth, but she judged that he would be able to stand it for a few seconds more, and made no move to relieve his discomfort.

'Put your hands on my waist – take my weight,' she rasped, as she brought her left hand down to join her right one.

Entering herself with two fingers, she used the other hand to massage her clitoris, drawing it out from under its protective hood and stroking its tip. The tiny scrap of flesh quivered beneath her touch, and she teetered on the very brink of ecstasy.

The plane was now circling the main airport as it waited for a landing spot to become available. Karen was aware that Justin felt it lose height, too, for he made a small noise of protest. She ignored him. Grinding her hips against her fingers, she felt all the pent-up tension of the past few days disintegrate, like the thousand shards of glass as a window is shattered, and scatter through her body like little pinpricks of bliss. All her senses focused on the small implosion centred in that tiny bundle of nerve-endings at the apex of her labia, to the exclusion of everything and everyone else.

Letting out her breath through her teeth in a low hiss of satisfaction, Karen pulled back abruptly. Justin gasped for air, his eyes wide as he watched her adjust her clothing. Karen could see the confusion in his eyes and felt a small twinge of compassion. After all, he had done everything he could to please her, had done everything she had asked, without question. He deserved some small reward.

Slowly, she reached out and ran her fingertips along the soft inside edge of his lower lip.

'Here,' she said softly, offering him the slick of honeyed dew on her fingertips.

The boy drew her fingers into his mouth hungrily, unzipping his trousers and reaching inside to touch his iron-hard prick. Karen smiled as she pulled her fingers out of his mouth, slowly.

'Good boy,' she whispered, leaning over to touch his cock.

Justin shuddered and let out a ragged sigh. Karen ran her hand once, twice along the silky-skinned shaft, then she straightened up.

'Happy wanking,' she murmured in his disbelieving ear, before leaving him alone in the toilet cubicle. Walking briskly back to her seat, she smiled at the air stewardess' disapproving expression at her late visit to the lavatory. Strapping herself in, she imagined the boy masturbating furiously in the toilet and knew he would use the memory of the experience as a trigger for arousal for months to come.

If she had had more time, she might have been inclined to arrange to meet him again, to explore his potential more fully. On another trip, she might well have done so, but this time she had other, more important things to think about.

Smiling, she settled back in her seat and prepared to land in Tierra del Sol. As soon as she stepped out into the balmy sunshine, the young steward was forgotten.

Ricardo was furious. Despite all his objections, Maria had still gone to dance for the tourists at the Casa the previous evening. Now she was eyeing him defiantly from across the bar, her hands on her hips, looking for all the world like their long-dead mother, if she only knew it. Ricardo deliberately hardened his heart, refusing to allow tender memories to soften his stance.

'I have told you, Maria, that you are not to dance the flamenco in public,' he raged now.

'And I have told *you*, brother dear, that I will do

as I damn well please! This is 1997, I am 22 years old and you have no right to tell me what I can and cannot do!'

'I am your brother!'

Maria sighed loudly, and Ricardo saw that there was love for him in her eyes beneath the fiery defiance.

'Yes, Ricardo, you are my brother. And I love you very, very much. But if you continue to try to run my life for me as you did when we were children, then I swear I will never speak to you again.'

'Maria!'

Ricardo stared at her, stunned. He barely recognised the beautiful, assertive young woman who stood before him, her soft brown eyes sharpened by her determination to have her own way. Where was the amenable child who had always looked up to him, who had been happy to be protected by her older brother? The transformation made him feel angry, sad, and not a little afraid. It was as if his whole world had shifted slightly, so that it now seemed out of focus, unfamiliar to him.

'I am sorry, Ricardo. I know you believe that you have my best interests at heart, but you are wrong to try to smother me.'

'What you need is a good husband to keep you in line!' he blustered, knowing as soon as the words fell from his lips that he had completely blown any credibility he might have had left with the sister he loved and worried over so very much.

Maria looked at him with a mixture of pity and

contempt. She spoke quietly, with a cool self-possession which impressed him, in spite of himself.

'What I need is for you to acknowledge my right to do whatever I choose. Because I love you, I would prefer to have your blessing, but I don't *need* it. Nor do I need your permission – '

'I'm not suggesting you need my permission. You don't understand, Maria – '

'Yes, I do understand,' she interrupted him quietly. 'But I don't agree.'

'But – '

'Goodbye, Ricardo – I need to go now and get ready for tonight's show.'

'Maria! Maria, come back here at once!'

Ricardo strode over to the door through which, seconds before, Maria had walked with such quiet dignity. He watched her walk away, her dark head held high, her back stiffened by pride, and he was aware of a sense of loss, of helplessness.

He didn't know what to do. How could he ever explain to Maria that he wanted to guide and protect her, not because he wanted to make her a prisoner of traditional values, as she seemed to think, but because he loved her and wanted to shield her from hurt? He was only too aware of the pain that could so casually be inflicted by the tourists who passed through Tierra de Sol.

'Oh, for God's sake!' he swore, turning away from the door in disgust.

To hell with modern women – what he needed was an old-fashioned girl to make his blood run hot and make him feel like a man again!

Chapter Three

Karen looked around her hotel room with little interest. Being reserved for Wingspan staff, it was sparsely furnished and situated at the back of the hotel right at the very top. There were no en suite facilities and the bathroom, which would doubtless be shared with some dozen other hotel staff, was at the end of a long and grimy corridor.

Karen did not even put down her bag. Getting out her mobile phone, she gazed out across the flat roof of the kitchens to the distant strip of dusty roadway visible from the window as she waited to be connected to London. There was no air conditioning and, within minutes, her entire body was bathed in sweat.

Aaron's voice was as clear as it would have been had he been standing in the room with her. She did not bother with pleasantries.

'What makes you think I'm going to live in this rathole all summer long?' she snapped.

'Karen? What do you mean?'

'I mean that if you think I'm going to swelter in this seedy little hotel when I'm doing *you* a favour, you can think again.'

'There must be some mistake, I promise you – '

'I don't want to hear any of your pathetic promises, Aaron,' Karen snapped, cutting him off in mid-sentence. 'I'm going out for a swim. I'll give you – ' she glanced at the slim gold watch on her wrist ' – three hours. If my accommodation arrangements haven't been changed to my satisfaction by then, I'm on the next plane home. Understand?' She broke the connection before he had time to reply.

She pictured him staring at the telephone receiver, and knew that her tone would have given him an erection. His handsome face would be stiff with tension and his hands would be shaking with the joy of humiliation.

Karen sighed. Poor sap! What would he do when she finally grew tired of him? Perhaps she should volunteer to give his fiancée some pointers. Whatever, so long as Aaron's current fierce need for her got her what she wanted, she wasn't going to waste time on compassion.

Leaving the hotel, she didn't give him another thought.

Ricardo eyed the fluffy-looking blonde sitting alone at the bar and knew he had found what he needed. She had come in with a group of high-spirited friends, with the first of the lunchtime crowd, and he had spotted her straight away. While her friends were noisy and raucous, this girl had the kind of demeanour which reminded Ricardo of a well-bred English lady, demure and modest, but not terrifically bright.

'Can I get you another drink?' he asked her, approaching her from the business side of the bar.

The girl looked up, her big, sherry-brown eyes reminding him of those of a startled fawn.

'I – yes, please.'

'Babycham, isn't it?' Ricardo said, already opening a bottle.

The girl nodded, glancing shyly at him from beneath her eyelashes, as if she wasn't too sure whether or not she ought to be speaking to him. Maybe her mother had warned her about predatory Latin men, he thought, smiling to himself.

'Your friends have all gone?' Ricardo said, when she had taken a sip.

Her small, pink tongue ran nervously along her lower lip, and he felt the first stirrings of sexual interest in the pit of his belly.

'Yes,' she replied, her voice so soft he had to lean forward to catch it. 'They've gone to the beach ... to meet some people they met last night.'

By 'people' Ricardo guessed that she meant men, and that this girl felt uncomfortable with the *en masse*, casual pick-up. Instinctively, he knew that she would not be unresponsive if he made a move on her, so long as he bided his time, won her trust. His desire for her sharpened as he contemplated the chase.

'My name is Ricardo Baddeiras – I am the owner

of the Bar del Amore.' He gave the small, smart half-bow which never failed to charm.

The girl giggled, hiding her mouth behind her hand.

'The bar of love! What a lovely name. So romantic! I'm Anita.'

She held out her hand and Ricardo took it in his. Instead of returning her handshake, he lifted it to his lips and planted a small, dry kiss on the back of it. Glancing at her from beneath his lashes, he saw her cheeks flush with pleasure, so he turned her hand over and kissed it again, in its very centre. This time he pressed the tip of his tongue lightly against the middle of her palm, feeling her jump at the light, erotic contact.

'I am charmed to meet you ... Anita,' he said, careful to use a Spanish inflection as he pronounced her name. English girls seemed to like the men they picked up in Tierra del Sol to be mysterious and exotic, and he was not averse to feeding their fantasies, especially not when it so often worked to his advantage.

Releasing Anita's hand, he pretended to busy himself polishing the clean glasses lined up under the bar.

'Are you here on holiday?' he asked her conversationally, after a few minutes.

Anita relaxed visibly as he steered her into harmless waters. Chatting desultorily, he gradually won her confidence. Over the next hour, he learnt that she lived in Croydon and had come on holiday with a group of workmates after a particularly traumatic split with the man she had been living with.

She worked as a junior manager in the credit control section of a large, multinational retail company and had few friends among the staff since her entire life had revolved around her boyfriend.

'Always dangerous, devoting your life to a man,' Ricardo said sagely, cynically playing on her need for him to be sensitive to her feelings.

'Exactly,' she said, looking at him with wonder and, he was pleased to see, a speculative gleam in her eyes.

It seemed that the girls with whom she had come away were no more than acquaintances, really, and she was uncomfortable with what seemed to be the main aim of their holiday – to sleep with as many men as was humanly possible in a fortnight.

'Sex for sex's sake is not always the best kind,' Ricardo said, sympathetically.

Anita giggled, again covering her mouth with her hand. This time, Ricardo gently moved it away.

'Don't hide your lovely smile,' he said softly, staring deeply into her eyes.

By this time, Anita was on her fourth Babycham, and her gaze on him was a little unfocused. He made a mental note to serve her with fruit juice next – he didn't mind her feeling mellow, but he didn't want to get her too drunk.

'You have a beautiful mouth,' he said now, his eyes caressing her lips which had parted softly.

He moved forward, as if to kiss her, then, when he was a breath away, he moved back, a regretful expression in his eyes.

'Forgive me – I meant no disrespect,' he said.

It was, even though he said it himself, a master stroke. Anita's light brown eyes widened, and her lips formed a small 'o' of dismay. Ricardo smiled inwardly as he watched her struggle with herself.

'I – I wouldn't be offended,' she said, so quietly he had to strain to hear her.

'No?' He raised one quizzical eyebrow. 'Then perhaps you would like to join me for lunch? I would like to get to know you better – very much.'

Anita stared at him. 'I know this probably sounds silly,' she said, 'but I feel as if I've known you for a long time.'

Seizing his chance, Ricardo leant forward, his expression intense. 'That's exactly how I feel about you, too,' he told her, dropping his voice an octave and making it reverberate with sincerity. 'From the moment you walked into the bar, I saw you, and I thought, I know this woman. Perhaps I am crazy too?' He laughed softly.

Anita, clearly entranced, shook her head in wonder. Ricardo smiled at her, disappointed that it had been so easy. She was undemanding enough company, though, and he decided to go through with his offer of lunch. There was something rather soothing about the way she was looking at him so adoringly. He was sorely in need of adoration after Maria's defiance.

Walking around to the front of the bar, he picked up Anita's hand and brushed his lips across the backs of her fingers. 'Shall we?' he asked.

She nodded and he saw in her eyes that she was in no doubt as to where lunch would lead.

* * *

62

Karen had half-forgotten how warm the Mediterranean sea could be. Swimming up and down the cove she remembered so well, she could, if she closed her eyes, imagine that time had slipped away, and that she was eighteen again, and in love for the first time.

Opening them again, she saw that the cove had been developed since the last time she had swum here with Ricardo. The steep cliff path had been replaced with a smooth, concrete pedestrian ramp, built to zigzag down the side of the cliff so that no section was too steep. Arranged on the beach were two regimented rows of white plastic sunloungers with gaily striped umbrellas between each, hireable by the half-day. In one corner, an enterprising local youth was hiring out pedaloes and inflatable dinghies. One of the latter floated aimlessly past her now, and she sighed, striking out for the shore.

Despite the commercialisation of the beach, it was still nowhere near as busy as the more popular south side of the island. Less than half of the sunloungers were occupied and there were no loud radios or noisy children to disrupt the peace and quiet.

Spurning the dubious comforts of a sunlounger, Karen braved the disapproving scowl of the man waiting to take her money, and spread her towel on the soft, pale sand. Lying back, she felt the sun on her wet skin and remembered.

'I will love you forever,' Ricardo had murmured, that first, wonderful day.

'Don't say that . . . not unless you really mean it,'

she had replied, putting her fingers softly against his lips. 'I couldn't bear it if you lied.'

'Never! Karen, I will never lie to you. I promise.'

His dark eyes had burned fiercely down at hers, his expression so intense, so sincere, that she could not help but believe him. But, then, she had wanted to believe him, to believe *in* him, so much . . .

'Oh! I'm so sorry!'

Karen sat up as a girl twisted over on her ankle and almost landed on top of her.

'Are you all right?' She could see that the girl was not, for her lovely face was screwed up in pain and she was clutching at her ankle. 'Here – let me see.'

The ankle was already swelling up, so Karen ran down to the water's edge to soak her spare towel in the waves. She wrung it out as she ran back to the girl, then applied the cool compress to the sprain.

'It should be ice-cold, but it'll do for the moment. Will you be all right while I run to the drinks bar over there for some ice?'

The girl glanced in the direction of Karen's nod. 'Of course. You are very kind. Thank you.'

'Just hold that towel on the swelling and raise up your leg – here, rest your foot on top of my bag.'

Minutes later, Karen was back with four cans of ice-cold cola, two of which she held against the swelling. The girl winced ruefully.

'I don't know what happened – I just seemed to roll over.'

'It's easily done in the sand. Would you like a drink? I bought two spare cans of cola.'

64

The girl grinned. 'Thank you. I'm Maria, and I hope that later you will allow me to buy you dinner, to thank you for your kindness.'

'There's really no need,' Karen protested, 'though I'd be glad of your company here on the beach. I'm Karen and I only just arrived today.'

'From England?'

'Yes. Have you ever been there?'

Maria's eyes took on a wistful expression as she looked out to sea.

'I have never even left the island. I live with my brother, you see, and he is very strict.

'I know!' she continued catching Karen's incredulous expression. 'In your country grown women of 22 do not listen to what their brothers say! I am trying not to, but it is hard. I love him very much, you see, and he has been good to me since our father died when I was ten. It's not so easy to be a liberated woman on Tierra del Sol!'

Karen laughed. 'I don't suppose it is.' She took a long draught of her cola. 'Tell me, Maria, what would you like to do if you were "liberated", as you call it?'

Maria shrugged her pretty, plump shoulders. 'It is nothing so scandalous. I like to dance the flamenco, but Rico, he thinks it is sinful to perform for the tourists. It is all right, of course, for him to sell them beer in his bar and take a new girl to his bed whenever he feels like it . . .' She shrugged again at the hopelessness of it all.

Karen stared at her, a suspicion forming in her mind. There was something hauntingly familiar about the shape of the girl's eyes . . .

'Where is this bar your brother owns?' she asked with feigned casualness.

'On the main road through Leventos. It is called the Bar del Amore.' She laughed, expecting Karen to be amused by the name, as were most of the English girls.

Forcing her lips into the ghost of a smile, Karen tried to recall the last time she had seen Maria Baddeiras. A shy wraith of a child, she had worn her long dark hair in two pigtails, and her big brown eyes had followed Karen everywhere she went. How strange that the first person she had met on arriving in Tierra del Sol should have been Ricardo's sister!

'Do you not remember me, Maria?' she asked softly.

Maria looked at her in surprise. 'Remember you? Have we met before?'

Karen nodded. 'A long, long time ago, when your father was alive – ' she could see the girl searching her face for clues, frowning in concentration. 'My hair was very long, then.'

'And you were a little bit plumper, and so pretty – not that you aren't pretty now, but I wanted so much to be like you then – oh, Karen, of course I remember you!'

To Karen's surprise, Maria embraced her, apparently genuinely pleased to see her again. But when she broke away a look of reproach shadowed her eyes.

'Ricardo was so upset when you left. You never said goodbye, Karen, not to me, not to Ricardo, you just disappeared, *poof!*'

66

Karen looked away quickly, remembered pain darkening her features. 'I had my reasons, Maria. You were only a child at the time, you wouldn't have understood.'

Maria touched her hand and, when Karen looked up quizzically at her, she smiled, the same soft smile Karen had remembered in the child.

'You should have said goodbye to me – children are not so easily left behind. I was hurt that you had thought so little of me that you did not want to say goodbye. As you say, I did not understand. But I think I might understand more now Karen.'

'I'm sorry if I hurt you, Maria – believe me, that was never my intention.'

'I know. I knew then, too.'

The two women smiled at each other in quiet complicity.

'So,' Maria said briskly, 'why have you come back?'

Karen explained briefly about the crisis with Wingspan, and Maria made a face.

'Oh dear, Karen, so you have come to make trouble for my brother, no?'

Karen was about to lie smoothly to reassure her, but found that she could not. 'Perhaps a little,' she admitted, with a wry grin.

'And you will enjoy this, no?'

'Of course not! Maria, what do you think I am?'

Maria regarded her with her solemn, dark eyes. 'I think you are a different girl to the one who left Tierra del Sol so long ago,' she said, with a certainty which shook Karen into silence. Then she smiled and the awkwardness dissipated.

'My brother deserves a little trouble. He has become – how do you say it? – too big for his shoes! I think we shall have fun together, you and I,' Maria said, struggling painfully to her feet. 'Now I must go back. Do you think you could help me up the cliff?'

'I can do better than that,' Karen replied, gathering up her things. 'I have a hire car at the top – I'll be glad to give you a lift back to the Bar del Amore.'

Maria glanced shrewdly at her.

'Are you sure, Karen?'

'Of course. Oh, please, Maria, take that look off your face! I have no lingering feelings towards your brother, I can assure you.'

'Really?' Maria said, linking her arm companionably through Karen's. 'I hope, then, that Ricardo will feel the same way.'

Karen looked at her sharply, but her face gave nothing away as she concentrated on hobbling across the soft sand.

Ricardo prepared to undress Anita with a sense of heightened anticipation. All through lunch he had been trying to imagine what her body would be like under the loose white shirt and pants she was wearing, and his imagination had removed her clothes over and over again.

Once she had established the parameters of their encounter – that what was about to happen between them was to be personal and private, no innuendoes in front of her friends, no empty promises of commitment – Anita had entered into the game

68

with an enthusiasm which had taken his breath away.

They were in one of the private rooms above the bar which the bar boys used on a nightly basis for their conquests. Before they had finished lunch, Ricardo had asked Darren to hide away anything crude or off-putting, such as the 'shagometer' which was normally pinned to the wall in the communal room. The boy had also been asked to ensure that there were clean sheets on the bed, and that the windows were opened to let in some fresh air. As far as Anita was concerned, this room might well have been his living quarters.

Now she trembled as his fingers skimmed the bare skin across her collarbones and he looked quizzically at her.

'What is it?' he asked, kindly.

She looked to be on the verge of tears and Ricardo had to suppress a flood of irritation. He would not be happy if she backed out now.

'It's – it's just that I've never . . . with anyone else. At least, not for a long time, before I met Michael . . .'

Ricardo relaxed. If all she was worried about was the fact that she'd been faithful to her boyfriend for so long, he knew he could overcome her reticence.

'It's all right, sweetheart, I understand. We will take things slowly, yes? And if there's anything you don't feel comfortable with – anything at all – you will tell me, and we will stop.' His voice was calm and understanding, whilst inside he was churning with impatience. Arranging his face into a picture of masculine tenderness, he tried another tack.

'Trust me, Anita. It will be good between us. Let me guide you along the path of love.'

He cringed inwardly as he gushed the over-the-top words, yet Anita seemed to fall for them. She swayed slightly towards him and, sensing her imminent capitulation, Ricardo kissed her, swallowing whatever words of protest might still be forming in her mind.

She clung to him, her fingers digging into his shoulders as he kissed her deeply, probing the barrier of her teeth with his tongue until they parted and he was granted access to the warmth within. She tasted sweet, like toffee, and he took his time, gently exploring the inside of her mouth.

Anita sighed and pressed herself against him, her soft, pillowy breasts pressing against the hardness of his chest. He could feel the heat of her body through the thin cotton of her blouse and he itched to tear it off her, to feel her naked skin against him.

Easy does it, he told himself. Instinct told him that, if he gave her the time she needed, Anita would be one hell of a good lay. He just had to take things at a pace at which she felt comfortable.

'It's hot today, is it not?' he murmured as he broke the kiss.

'I can feel how hot you are,' she replied, running her hands over the front of his shirt.

Ricardo stood very still, allowing her confidence to grow as she traced the musculature of his chest with her palms. Glancing at him to gauge his reaction, she began to unbutton his shirt.

'Ooh – I love hairy men!' she said with a smothered giggle as she saw his chest.

'I don't bite,' he said playfully, capturing her hand and bringing it up to his chest.

Her fingers ran lightly – too lightly – over the whorls of hair.

'Firmer,' he said, showing her by holding her hand again. 'I am very ticklish!'

She laughed, and he knew that this was the way to paradise, so long as he took things slowly and playfully, biding his time. His interest quickened as he realised that sex with her was not going to be quite as straightforward as he had assumed it would be, after all.

He reached for her and drew her close, feeling the shape of her body under her loose blouse. She was plumper than he had at first thought, but not unattractively so. Her curves were soft and cherubic, her skin silky under his fingertips, sensitive to every caress.

'Let me take this off,' she murmured huskily.

Ricardo waited as she unbuttoned her blouse. His fingers itched to help her, but he guessed that she would feel more comfortable, more in control if he continued to allow her to set the pace – at least for now.

She was wearing a white satin *balconette* type bra which pushed her breasts up and together. Ricardo's eyes roamed the creamy globes appreciatively. Glancing at Anita's face, he judged her ready for him to take a more proactive role in their encounter.

'So beautiful,' he murmured, dipping his head to place a small, chaste kiss on each curvaceous mound. 'So womanly.'

He felt Anita tremble as he buried his face in the

warm valley between them, flicking his tongue over the surface of her skin. It tasted of the piquant salt of fresh sweat, underlined by a sweetness which was all her own. Encouraged by her compliance, Ricardo began to kiss her – wet, open-mouthed kisses that sucked at her skin.

Anita moaned softly and her hands steadied her against his shoulders.

'Oh, Ricardo,' she gasped. 'I love it . . .'

Realising that she was clearly a woman who enjoyed her breasts as much as he was about to, Ricardo reached around to unclip the bra. Freed from their restraint, her breasts burst out into his waiting hands, the abundant flesh quivering against his palms.

Sucking and kissing Anita's breasts was a sensual delight Ricardo had not bargained for. As his lips moved over her skin she moaned and quivered, her breasts seeming to take on a life of their own as they moved under his hands.

Her nipples were like two hard little pips as he rolled them against his tongue and he felt the tension grip her as she reached a small climax, brought about purely by his stimulating them. The ease with which she reached orgasm excited him, and he moved to take off her trousers, eager to touch and taste the evidence of her satisfaction.

As he had expected, the gusset of her panties was soaked with her juices. She gasped as his fingers worked their way under the elastic and sank into the hot, pulpy flesh of her sex.

'Oh – oh yes!' she hissed, wiggling her hips so

that her vulva was squashed against his fingertips. 'Give it to me . . .'

'I intend to,' Ricardo muttered as he manoeuvred her so that the backs of her knees were touching the edge of the bed, 'believe me, I intend to!'

Anita squealed as he pushed her gently on to the bed and she lost her balance, landing on her back with a bump. Ricardo followed her, covering her upper body with his own, pinning her to the bed. With one hand, he grasped her wrists and dragged her arms up above her head. Anita's eyes widened as she realised she couldn't move.

'Ricardo – '

'Ssh!' He smothered her token protest with a long kiss, his fingers entering her and moving in a circular motion just inside her vagina. His thumb rasped with deliberate carelessness across the sensitised tip of her clitoris and she cried out against his mouth.

Ricardo responded by biting her lower lip, the harsh little nip making her jump, taking her mind off the smaller pain of his digital ministrations. He wanted her to squirm underneath him, to put up some resistance – no matter how illusory – to his possession of her.

Anita's discomfort was clearly not altogether faked, for the fingers of the hand which held her wrists bit into her skin and his lips were no longer gentle against her throat. He used his fingers mercilessly, penetrating her with three of them and spreading them slightly to open and stretch her.

She moaned and writhed beneath him, and her movements spurred him on, inflaming his desire until he felt his erection would burst through his trousers and penetrate her by instinct alone.

'Do it properly, Ricardo,' she whispered urgently against his hair. 'Give it to me hard and strong.'

A part of him wondered at the transformation in her as he released her hands, pulling his fingers roughly out of her so that he could attend to unfastening his flies.

Anita lay before him, breathing heavily, her pleasantly plump body very white against the navy blue sheets. When he was naked, Ricardo gave in to the urge to flip her over on to her belly. Anita gave a small cry of shock as he lifted her with one hand splayed across her stomach, so that her buttocks were presented to him in all their tempting, sumptuous glory.

'Lift it up higher,' he said, pressing his lips against her ear, 'show me what a bad girl you can be.'

He had read her perfectly. With a small sob of shame, Anita pushed her fleshy backside up, pressing her face into the pillows as she waited to see what he would do. The smack of his palm across her bottom cheeks was very loud in the small room, louder even than the shocked cry which escaped from between Anita's lips.

'I can see how bad you are,' Ricardo said, his voice low and compelling. 'I can see how moist and shiny you are.'

'Oh, oh yes, I am bad,' she whispered, 'please – please punish me for my wickedness.'

Ricardo obliged happily, reddening her bottom with the palm of his hand, all the while aware of his erection growing stiffer and straighter, until he felt he would come all over her heated flesh.

'You are so wet, so ready for a cock. It could be any cock, couldn't it Anita? Any man will do, just so long as something fills that hungry, wet hole . . .'

'Ahh!' she cried as he spanked her again. 'Please – no more. I can't bear it!'

'Can't? Or won't?' he asked, pausing to caress her burning flesh with the palm of his hand. 'What is it you want, then, Anita?'

'I want you to fuck me,' she whispered.

'Like this? From behind?'

'Yes. Any way, any way at all, only please, please fuck me!'

Ricardo pretended to consider, enjoying the game. 'Perhaps I should punish you some more first, for your impertinence. Yes, that might be a good idea.'

'No! Please, please, I'm begging you.'

Ricardo liked the sound of her begging, it fitted his need of her very well. Taking his cock in his hand, he stroked it thoughtfully as he rolled a condom along its length, gazing at her spread buttocks in anticipation.

The reddened, wet purse of her sex hung temptingly between her legs, enticing him to enter her. Above it, the rosy hole of her anus was also spread wide, tempting, but less amenable. He decided to go for her quim.

Anita cried out as he entered her with one sure, accurate stroke, sinking into her hot, wet flesh until his balls touched her labia.

'Is this what you wanted?' he gasped, losing his

grip on the game as the silky, pleated tube sent delightful rippling sensations along the length of his shaft.

'Harder!' she cried, lost in the moment as she bucked her hips back against him. 'Make it harder – faster!'

Ricardo obliged, hammering into her like a man possessed. This was what he needed, this mindless, animal rutting that served, for a few moments at least, to drive everything out of his mind except the relentless, obsessive drive towards orgasm.

Anita's body squirmed wildly beneath his as the force of his thrusting rocked it, causing her abundant flesh to ripple and shake. Her buttocks glowed where he had spanked them, and he could feel the heat against his belly. Knowing that he was causing her discomfort by rubbing against her punished flesh excited him in a way which made him feel a little ashamed.

She made no objection, though, and so Ricardo put his darker thoughts aside, living in the moment. He could feel the tension in her as she, too, strove towards climax, and he reached down between her legs to rub the swollen nub of her clitoris to speed her on her way.

He wanted her to come first, as if that was some small victory, male over female, though by definition but a fleeting triumph. As Anita's body catapulted into orgasm, her vaginal walls convulsed wildly, milking his pumping cock so that it would no longer have been possible to hold back even had he wanted to.

It was enough, though, that he had chased and

caught her: enough that he had driven her to beg and plead for his cock. As he came, Ricardo cried out – an incoherent, atavistic whoop of joy that he had found a woman to restore his bruised male pride, a woman who was happy to acknowledge his dominion over her.

Chapter Four

'Tell me, is the Bar del Amore as unruly as the last Wingspan rep seemed to think?' Karen asked Maria as she drove along the winding coast road.

She felt Maria's perceptive eyes on her and wondered if the girl could see through her casual question. Maria's reply confirmed that she could.

'What you mean is, is Ricardo a part of it?' Maria sighed. 'I am sorry to say that my brother is not an honourable man when it comes to the ladies.'

'Was he ever?' Karen muttered bitterly.

Maria put her hand over Karen's briefly as it rested on the steering wheel.

'You have to understand the temptations of doing a job like his. So many beautiful women, new ones coming week after week, many throwing themselves at him – he's not a saint, you know.'

Karen shook her head, making a small noise of disgust at the back of her throat.

'Maria, that's like saying that a jeweller's is full of desirable things, so I couldn't be blamed for shop-lifting. Or that if you carry a purse which bulges full of money a thief has the right to steal it.'

Maria laughed softly. 'Perhaps,' she conceded. 'Karen, why don't you come to the bar tonight, and see for yourself?'

Karen glanced at her.

'All right. In the meantime, would you have dinner with me? I have a small business venture I'm trying to get off the ground and I think you might be able to help me with it.'

'I'm intrigued. Okay – I'm all yours.'

Karen drove past the turning which would have taken them to Leventos, heading instead for the hotel. The manager at the reception desk gave every appearance of having been waiting for her.

'*Señorita*, I am so sorry for the misunderstanding when you arrived. I have taken the liberty of transferring your belongings to a private villa by the beach – if you would like to follow me?'

Karen got back into her car and followed the manager as he led the way in his ageing Seat. They took a long private road which meandered away from the main tourist route, and towards the shore. The villa was small but beautifully appointed, and Karen wondered who Aaron had had to bribe, or bully, to get it for her.

'Very nice,' Maria said, echoing her thoughts.

'Hmm. It'll do,' Karen said, dismissing the hotel manager with a cool nod.

When he had gone, she turned to Maria and

grinned. 'This is an improvement on the grotty room Wingspan originally expected me to have!'

'How did you do it?' Maria asked curiously.

'Oh, I pulled a few strings in London.' Karen was non-committal as she opened all the doors and inspected each room.

The villa comprised a central living-cum-dining room with a small galley kitchen leading off it, which was fitted with every modern convenience she might conceivably need. Another door opened on to a single bedroom, small but prettily furnished, with its own tiny en suite facilities. The main bedroom contained a low double bed, and a suite of pristine white furniture. A long window along one wall provided an uninterrupted view of the ocean, facing East, so she would be able to watch the sun rising over the horizon.

'Wow – this looks like a jacuzzi,' Maria said from the bathroom leading off the main bedroom.

Glancing in, Karen saw that she had been provided with a larger than average corner bath which doubled as a whirlpool, a wash basin and vanity unit, and a bidet as well as the lavatory.

'I think I'll be quite comfortable here, don't you?' she said, smiling at Maria with a twinkle in her eye.

Maria laughed.

'I think so. Shall we eat dinner here, or go out?'

'Go out, I think, then we can make our way to the bar. Would you wait while I unpack and change? Make yourself at home.' Karen unzipped her case, aware of Maria's speculative glance at her as she left the room. There was no doubt about it, there were no flies on Maria – much as Karen liked her, and much as the girl seemed to support Karen's intention to take her brother to task, she was still Ricardo's sister. Karen decided to be safe rather than sorry; she would be careful to hide her motives from Maria in the future.

Ricardo and Anita emerged from the upstairs flat just as the bar was beginning to fill up. Hot, perspiring and satisfied, Ricardo offered to let her have the first shower before he got himself ready for the evening.

'I'll wait for you, shall I?' Anita asked, her big, sherry-brown eyes wide and anxious.

Suppressing a dart of irritation, Ricardo nodded. 'If you like. I'll see you at the bar – tell Darren I said he was to get you a drink on the house.'

He could see that she was disappointed that what little intimacy they had shared had evaporated the moment they had left the bed. The sheets lay in disarray, empty condom wrappers littered the floor, and the smell of sex and her cigarette smoke, permeated the little room.

'Ask Darren to send someone up to tidy the place, would you?' he called after her, as she went reluctantly down the stairs.

Stepping under the shower, he turned the dial to hot, eager to scrub every trace of her from his body. He always seemed to feel like this after sex this days – empty, spiritually if not physically dissatisfied, and strangely depressed.

He couldn't stand the clinginess afterwards. As far as he was concerned, they had enjoyed great sex for an afternoon, and that was it, the extent of their relationship. It had already run its natural course, so what was the point in prolonging it with social niceties?

Anita would be the type to expect him to stay by her side all evening, as some kind of signal to the world at large that she was special to him in some way, worthy of its respect. What was it with women? Didn't any of them have a healthy level of self-esteem?

Ricardo took his time in the shower, shaving, and washing and drying his hair before dressing in clean blue jeans and a precision-pressed white shirt. He always kept a supply of fresh clothes at the bar for just this kind of eventuality.

Music filtered up the stairs as the bar began to fill with early evening revellers, and the upstairs flat became crowded as his bar boys arrived for work.

'Keep the noise down, eh?' he said mildly as he came out of the bedroom, and they all turned to look at him as if they were surprised to see him there. 'Good crowd downstairs, yes?'

'Looks like it's going to be a good night, boss,' Jamie, one of his English bar boys, replied.

Ricardo nodded. 'That's good. I want you to be extra careful for the next few days – give the ladies what they want, but be sure that no one is offended, before, during, or after. I'm expecting the new Wingspan representative to pay us a visit when she, or he, arrives. We need Wingspan's goodwill and, as you know, that's been tested recently.' He glanced significantly at Gunter, the bar boy responsible for the latest complaint. 'Be discreet, OK?'

They dispersed amidst mumbling and subdued laughter. As they all filed downstairs, Ricardo stopped Jamie.

'What can I do for you, boss?' the boy asked in his irrepressibly cheerful East London accent.

'There's a girl at the bar – blonde, dizzy looking – take care of her for me, would you? See to it that she gets back to her hotel all right.'

'Sorted, boss. See you later.'

Ricardo gave him five minutes to get downstairs and engage Anita in conversation, then he, too, went down to the bar, confident that she would be sufficiently distracted to allow him to get on with his night's work.

Karen and Maria took their time over dinner. As they talked, they discovered a rapport which delighted Karen – she had resigned herself to missing her female friends while she was away for the summer, and she was glad to have found someone with whom she seemed to have something in common.

Maria told her about her problems with Ricardo and her love of the flamenco.

'You know, you could always use the spare room at the villa if ever you feel the need to get away,' Karen offered. 'I'm only supposed to be here for six months, so it would only be a temporary solution, but you're more than welcome if you think it might give you some breathing space.'

Maria regarded her thoughtfully. 'You know, that might not be a bad idea. Can I leave it open?'

'Sure. Just turn up, any time.'

Calling the waiter over, Karen ordered a second glass of wine to be poured, and they drank a toast to cement the agreement.

'You know,' said Maria, after a few minutes, 'I have been talking about myself all evening – you were going to tell me about a business venture, I think, yes?'

Karen nodded. 'That's right. I have a – an acquaintance who wants to buy a plot of land for a hotel. I thought Leventos might be a good place to look.'

'Sure, but the planning rules are becoming tighter now that Tierra del Sol is beginning to develop. If you bought land now, or even a property which you could convert, it could easily be months before the necessary permits are granted. You know how slowly these things work here – *mañana*, always *mañana*.' She shrugged.

'It would take a good nine to twelve months to carry out repairs and building work.'

'Yes. Of course, if you bought a place which had already been granted permission, you could set up straight away.'

Karen looked at her quizzically as she picked up on something in her tone.

'Do you know of such a place?

Maria's eyes sparkled with mischief.

'I might. Come, let me show you before we go to the Bar del Amore. It might be completely unsuitable, but . . .' She moved her hand in a rocking motion from side to side.

Karen followed her out of the restaurant, intrigued. She drove north again, towards Leventos.

Maria was infuriatingly tight-lipped about the site they were going to see.

'I want you to judge for yourself,' was all she would say.

Karen spotted the Bar del Amore as soon as they turned into the main street. Loud music was playing and bright lights patterned the concrete pavement outside it with spangled panes of colour. A tall, amicable youth with dark blond hair tied in a loose ponytail was luring prospective customers into the place with a combination of seductive charm and an offer of free cocktails.

'That's Gunter,' Maria said as they drove past.

'The insensitive pig who led that young girl on?' Karen said.

'That's him. Park over here, to the right.'

Karen parked the car and joined Maria on the pavement. 'I thought you wanted me to see this development site?' she said.

'This is it.'

Karen looked around her. All she could see were the usual tourists traps, and a run-down clapboard building, unlit, which looked like a dull brown sparrow in a line of tawdry peacocks. Then she saw the FOR SALE sign nailed to the front of it.

'*This* is it?'

Maria laughed at her incredulity.

'It is a prime site. Ricardo wants to buy it so that he can expand the Bar del Amore, but the owner won't sell. He and our father fell out many years ago and he seems to have transferred his ill feeling on to Ricardo.'

'So why would he sell to me, a total stranger, and a foreigner to boot?'

'He wouldn't.' Maria fixed her with an unwavering gaze. 'But he would sell to me.'

'To you? But – I don't understand . . .?'

'This place, it used to be a bar and restaurant. If you buy it, you could open it as a bar straight away while your friend applies for the necessary permits to change it into a hotel.'

'A bar? In direct competition with your brother?'

'Why not? We could provide a place for women to drink and have fun without any danger of exploitation by Ricardo's bar boys.'

'And what would you get out of it, Maria?'

The other girl shrugged. 'I would be able to dance. And I am experienced at running a bar – I could help you. Just for this summer, Karen. It would be fun, don't you think?'

Karen stared thoughtfully at her. Whatever the girl's motives were for defying her brother, it was a good idea.

'Let's come back in daylight to have a look around,' she suggested. 'I'd have to put together a report and some ideas for my friend, though – he might not buy into it.'

Maria was satisfied. 'I'm sure you would be able to persuade him, Karen,' she said brightly. 'Shall we go over to the bar?'

They walked across the street, Maria still limping slightly on her sprained ankle. 'Good evening, Gunter,' she said, as they passed the boy on the door.

'Hi, Maria. Who is your friend?'

He regarded Karen with a quickening interest. She glared at him and saw a spark in the back of his eyes which responded readily to her high-handedness. So, Gunter the sex-god seems to be something of a submissive, she thought to herself, filing the information away for future reference.

An idea was taking shape in her mind, triggered by Maria's proposal. An idea so preposterous that it took her breath away.

'Maria . . .' her voice trailed away as she saw that Maria was heading towards a tall, dark-haired man who was standing at the bar. The blood drained from her face and her legs seemed to turn to jelly as she recognised Ricardo.

He was bigger than she remembered him, broader, but then he must be thirty, now, a mature man. His hair, however, was still as thick and glossy as she remembered it, though now it was cut close to his head, probably by an expensive stylist. The brightness of his shirt showed off the caramel tan of his skin, and a vivid image assaulted her, of herself licking every inch of that smooth, bronzed flesh.

He turned as Maria reached him and Karen saw that his face had grown more angular, more manly over time. She recognised the concern in his face as he saw that Maria was limping, and watched as he took his sister by the arms and shook her slightly, as if angry with her for injuring herself.

Then, as if in slow motion, Karen saw Maria nod towards her, and Ricardo raised his head, looking straight at her.

* * *

It was her, and yet it wasn't her. Ricardo felt the blood slow in his veins as he realised that Maria was right. Karen was standing in his bar, staring at him as if she had seen a ghost.

Her black hair was cropped short in a severe, spiky style that, he had to admit, set off her elfin face to perfection. How often he had dreamt of that sweet, heart-shaped face, that pale, pale skin, and the wide, violet eyes which gazed at him now with an expression he could not read.

Automatically, he stepped towards her, wanting to look into her eyes and read her mind.

'Karen!'

She inclined her head slightly.

'Ricardo.'

His eyes scanned her face, but her expression remained inscrutable, unreadable. Close to, he imagined he could feel the warmth of her body, smell the sweet, feminine fragrance of her skin. The memory was sharp, vivid, even after all these years, and he wondered if she might possibly be harbouring similar memories of him.

'What are you doing here?' he asked her.

The ghost of a smile passed across her features, a shadow of the happy grin he had held close in his heart.

'Didn't Maria tell you?' she said, and her voice was just as he remembered it. 'I'm the new Wingspan rep – I've come to get you to clean up your act.'

Ricardo gazed at her, momentarily dumbstruck. Then he threw back his head and roared with laughter.

'This amuses you?' Karen asked, coolly, when he stopped.

'Ah, Karen,' he said, his eyes soft as they roamed her face. 'You must admit, it is an irony, no? That it was you, of all people, who was sent to slap my wrists?'

Karen smiled grimly. 'Not at all, Ricardo – I asked to come.'

She saw that she had surprised him, and was glad to have pierced his aura of smugness.

'You did? Why?'

She fixed him with her unwavering glance, noting with satisfaction that her directness excited him.

'Because you are out of order, Ricardo. You've gone too far.'

If her words unnerved him, he did not show it. Instead, he stepped closer to her, so close that she could feel the heat of him, could sense the sexual tension in the way he held himself.

'Do you really believe that, darling?' he murmured, for her ears only.

Karen felt a sudden, unwelcome dart of desire. She hadn't bargained on wanting him still. Nowadays, when she felt this sudden, hot, liquid rush in the presence of a man, she took him to her bed and fucked it out of her system. Maybe that's what she should do now, with Ricardo.

'I am not the same as I was ten years ago,' she said, the huskiness in her voice betraying her.

She could smell the scent of his skin, a scent she remembered only too well. Her own weakness appalled her, made her want to lash out at him.

Instead, she stood her ground, waiting for him to reply.

'I can see that,' he said, running his eyes over her cropped hair and the determined set of her jaw. 'You are – your own woman, yes?'

The remark was made lightly, but to Karen it sounded like a challenge. She gazed into the deep, dark pools of his eyes, and for a moment she was eighteen again, emotionally at his mercy. It was not a comfortable feeling.

Ricardo recognised how she felt, and smiled softly. 'I have never forgotten you, darling.' He touched her hair lightly, an expression of genuine pain passing across his features as she flinched away. He allowed his arm to drop back to his side. 'Why did you leave Tierra del Sol the way you did? Without saying goodbye?'

Karen realised she was swaying imperceptibly towards him and brought herself up short.

'Some things are better left unsaid,' she told him curtly, clenching her fists at her sides to stop herself from touching him.

'And some things should never have been left unsaid,' he said, quietly.

Karen felt a pulse of remembered desire, mixed with pain, move through her. Instinct told her that, for once in his life, Ricardo was being sincere. Then the familiar, roguish look came back on to his face, and the moment passed.

'Come – have a drink with me. Then maybe later we can remind ourselves of that summer long ago, yes?'

Karen bit back the sharp retort which sprang to

her lips and followed him to the bar. His shoulders were broad beneath his white shirt and his buttocks were taut and infinitely touchable. He wanted her, that much was plain, and she knew, emotion aside, that she wanted him. Why not? she thought grimly to herself. She'd taken other men to her bed without fancying them half as much as she did Ricardo. So, why the hell not?

Ricardo drove quickly along the winding country lanes and Karen found it difficult to keep up with him in the darkness, as she trailed his headlights doggedly. He hadn't been happy when she had refused to leave her car in Leventos, and she guessed that this display of macho behaviour was designed to signal his displeasure.

She laughed aloud, buoyed up by the adrenalin coursing through her veins. She was going to fuck Ricardo. Not be seduced by him, as he obviously thought, or make love with him, as she had fondly assumed they used to do before, but fuck him senseless. It would be a meeting of equals, this time, two sexual predators battling for supremacy.

Afterwards, she would take great pleasure in destroying his business and the cosy little life he had made for himself in Leventos, and all with the help of his loving sister. It was perfect! She couldn't wait to see his face when he realised that, meta-phorically speaking this time, she had fucked him again!

Ricardo lived with Maria in his father's house by the sea. It looked like a castle from a gothic fairytale, silhouetted against the violet-black skyline as Karen drove up to the steps. Getting out of her car, she could hear the sound of the waves crashing on the rocks below, and she shivered. They seemed to have a rhythm, like the beating of her heart.

She could smell the strong ozone scent of sea salt and she breathed in deeply, filling her lungs with the clean air.

He had opened the door and was waiting for her. As she looked up at him, framed by the doorway, she felt a *frisson* of tension. He looked mean and moody, like the personification of a hero in a romantic novel. The Spanish landowner in his castle. Karen was almost disappointed with herself for finding him so infinitely attractive, though it did cross her mind that he should have been dressed all in black, not in his whiter-than-white shirt and freshly laundered jeans.

The whimsical turn of her thoughts unnerved her, made her feel unsure of herself. It was not a feeling she was used to, and she certainly did not like it.

Inside, it looked as though he hadn't changed anything since his father had died. The decor reminded Karen of a spartan baronial seat: the floorboards in the main room were polished, and bare save for an almost threadbare patterned rug in the centre of them. The walls were half-panelled in a dark wood, and the effect would have been claustrophobic if the ceilings hadn't been so high. There were three spindle-legged sofas upholstered in thin red mouflon, arranged in a 'U' shape around the vast fireplace, and a slightly musty, unlived-in smell hung in the air, making her want to sneeze.

Ricardo lit a fire and within a few minutes flames were leaping up the chimney. Their light and heat transformed the room, making it look warm and welcoming.

'Can I get you a drink? Some brandy – or there may be some wine?'

'Brandy will be fine, thank you.'

Karen took the balloon glass from him and swilled the amber liquid absently around the bowl. 'This is like something out of a film set! Do you and Maria really live here?'

Ricardo glanced around the room as if seeing it with her eyes. 'I spend much of my time at the bar,' he said.

'Leaving Maria here on her own?' Karen could not imagine that it was a comfortable place for a young girl to have grown up, virtually alone.

'We have a housekeeper; Maria is not often alone,' he replied defensively. 'Besides, she is not coming home tonight, she is staying with an old schoolfriend in Leventos.'

He smiled as he sat next to her on the middle sofa.

'So, we're all alone, are we, Ricardo?'

'Yes. All alone until morning.'

Karen sipped from her glass, watching him closely over the rim. 'You were very sure that I would come back here with you,' she said.

He shrugged. 'You were very sure that I would ask you.'

'*Touché.*' She laughed.

'You still laugh in the same way,' Ricardo said

softly. 'The more time I spend with you, the more I see that which has not changed.'

His observation did not please Karen, and she frowned.

'You are quite wrong, Ricardo, there is nothing about me that is remotely the same as the girl you remember – Oh!'

He cut her off by swooping on her lips, taking her glass from her hand as he pulled her close to him. Karen's protests were swallowed as he probed her mouth with his tongue, seeking out the most sensitive areas and raking the inside of it as if he wanted to taste all of her at once. They were both breathless when they broke apart.

'That has not changed,' he said, his voice ragged. 'You still want me as much as you ever did.'

His arrogance took Karen's breath away. Without thinking about what she was doing, she raised her hand to slap his face.

'Why, you – '

'*No*, Karen.'

He caught her wrist easily and, with one deft movement, unbalanced her so that she fell against him. Though she struggled, she could not prevent him from kissing her again. She was determined not to succumb to the pleasure this time and, as soon as she could gain purchase, she bit him on the lower lip.

'Ah!' he pulled back in shock, and Karen saw that she had drawn a tiny amount of blood.

Glancing reproachfully at her, Ricardo put his fingers to his lips. His eyes widened as he saw the blood smearing them, and the look he gave her made the hairs on the back of her neck stand up.

'Ricardo – '

'My God! You have turned into a hellcat!'

He reached for her again and they rolled together off the settee and on to the stringy mat on the floor. As though their movements had been choreographed, Karen landed on top of Ricardo, and she quickly centred her weight so that she was straddling his hips rendering him helpless. A surge of arousal seared her as she recognised the power she had over him, and it was made more intense by the look of surprise in his eyes.

'Karen – '

'Shut up! I'm going to fuck you, Ricardo, fuck you like you've never been fucked before! But, if you dare to try to pull some macho stunt and overpower me, I'll be out of that door like lightning. Do you understand me?'

'Perfectly, darling – now will you let me up so that I can take off my clothes?'

She saw in his eyes that her threats amused him, but she reined in her temper. Right now she needed him to assuage the fierce lust that had ignited in her the moment she had seen him. Later, she would teach him not to laugh at her. All in good time.

Karen watched as he stripped off his clothes, her mind cataloguing the way his body had changed from adolescence to adulthood. He was broader, of course, and the planes of his body were harder, more defined. His chest was covered with a thick mat of dark hair, arrowing downward and disappearing into the waistband of his jeans.

She licked her lips as she tracked the movement of his fingers, slipping one button through at a time, until his jeans hung open, exposing a pair of plain white shorts which barely contained his erection.

Could it be that the beautiful twenty-year-old cock she remembered had actually matured and grown? She had thought her memories of it were vivid, fresh, but nothing could have prepared her for the beauty of it as he rolled down his shorts.

Ricardo saw the pleasure in her eyes as she gazed at him, and his own eyes darkened.

'What is it?' he queried, standing before her in all his naked, masculine glory.

Karen shook her head, smiling. 'I'm not going to make you any more conceited than you already are. Do you remember how best to use that thing?' She nodded towards his penis which was standing proud, pointing up towards his heart.

'Take off your clothes, Karen,' he said gruffly, 'and I'll show you.'

Karen wanted him to stop talking, to show her by his actions rather than his words that he remembered her. She undressed slowly, aware of the effect she was having on him, and revelling in it. Ricardo was clearly finding it difficult to keep from grabbing at her and taking her there and then, but he also seemed mindful of her threat to walk out if he jumped on her, and so he contented himself, for now, with watching her.

'So,' she said, as she stood naked in front of the fire, mere feet away from him, 'do you still say I haven't changed?'

She was proud of her body, knew it to be worthy

of devotion, and she displayed herself in front of Ricardo without compunction. His eyes were hot as he ran them over her from top to toe, and Karen imagined, just as she had done the first time he had seen her naked, that her skin tingled wherever his gaze fell.

After what seemed to Karen to be an eternity, he shook his head. 'I was wrong, my darling, you *have* changed. Before, you were a lovely girl, but now you are a woman beyond compare.'

Karen shivered, whether at his words, or at a sudden chill in the room, she neither knew nor cared. She only knew that, at that moment, she wanted him with a sudden, unwelcome tenderness she thought had died within her when she had left him ten years before. Her desire to overcome him, to make their coming together a battle, slipped away as she read her own need mirrored in Ricardo's eyes.

As if by telepathy, they moved towards each other, and Ricardo drew her into the circle of his arms. His skin was warm against hers, and achingly familiar, and she leant against him, wanting to absorb the essence of him.

'Karen . . .' he murmured against her hair, transporting her back in time, turning her weak with old, remembered longings.

With a small, incoherent sound at the back of her throat, Karen pressed him close to her, wanting to imprint the feel of his body against hers on her memory for a second time. His erection pressed urgently against the soft mound of her belly and she felt her womanhood respond, moistening and opening in readiness for him.

Together, they sank on to the rug, hands and lips exploring, eyes communicating in a language far more intimate than either could have managed conventionally. Karen wanted nothing more than to feel him inside her again, to be as one with him, truly possessed, as she knew she never had been since.

Ricardo muttered endearments in his own tongue as he dipped his head to kiss her breasts, her shoulders, her wrists and her stomach. Karen felt herself tense as his lips sought and found the moist cleft of her sex, and cried out with need as his tongue explored her folds, reacquainting itself with the taste and texture of her most intimate flesh.

She shifted restlessly, meshing her fingers in his hair to lift his head, trying to transmit to him her urgent need for possession. Ricardo did not object when she manoeuvred him on to his back and straddled him again, this time holding his arms up above his head in a pose of mock submission.

She knew he was only humouring her, as if she needed any confirmation, by the dark glitter in his eyes. He was allowing her to take the lead for now, but Karen was very aware that he would only allow it for as long as *he* wished. It was a novel proposition for her to be with a man whose sexual leanings did not incline towards the submissive, and she found, to her disgust, that she was enjoying the feeling that, for once, she was not wholly responsible for both her own, and the man's pleasure. Ricardo Baddeiras was too much of a traditional man to allow his woman to take the initiative for long.

Karen decided to make the best of his complaisance while it lasted. Raising her hips, she positioned herself directly above his cock, so that it nudged at the entrance to her body. She could feel the tension in him, mirroring her own as she guided the tip of his penis into her again, then sat down on him, causing him to slide into her.

She sat still for a moment, relishing the sensation of having him inside her at last. Ricardo eased his hand in between their bodies and found her clitoris with unerring accuracy. The effect was electrifying. Waves of climax rolled through from Karen's clitoris, causing her vagina to convulse and bathe him in her honeyed juices. She cried out, angry with him for bringing on her climax so soon, yet unable to hold back.

Giving in, she ground her pubis against his, rocking her hips back and forth to give him maximum penetration. It gave her some small satisfaction to prevent him from thrusting into her, as he so clearly wanted to do. She pinned him down so that he was utterly incapable of movement – totally at her mercy at last.

Though he groaned in protest, and tried to move her so that he could flip her over on to her back, Karen resisted, holding him fast with her thigh muscles and bringing him to a climax purely by the action of the deeper, more intimate muscles inside her.

Ricardo cried out her name as he came, just as he had always used to, and at the moment of fulfilment,

Karen was suddenly beset by an inexplicable sadness. Transmuting that emotion into a steely anger, she squeezed his cock with her internal muscles, milking him dry, and not stopping until he grasped her by the hips and, with a gargantuan effort, rolled with her so that they were lying, still entwined, face to face on the rug.

'Ssh,' he said, touching her cheek with gentle fingers.

It was only then that Karen realised that she was crying. This uncharacteristic display of weakness made her so angry that she pulled abruptly away from him and scrambled to her feet.

Ricardo rose more slowly, and stood watching her impassively as she pulled on her clothes.

'Karen,' he said as she picked up her car keys and made for the door. 'Karen, don't leave like this – '

'Don't tell me what to do!' she said, whirling on him viciously.

'I don't understand – I thought – '

'That I would be a pushover? That we could really simply carry on where we left off? Grow up, Ricardo, and accept that things will never be the same again!'

She slammed the door after her, carrying with her his expression of total bewilderment.

Chapter Five

*A*ll that night, Karen lay awake, myriad thoughts circling around in her head. It wasn't that she couldn't get Ricardo out of her mind, she told herself fiercely, more that there was so much to be done, so many plans to make.

Maria's suggestion that she should buy the building almost opposite Ricardo's had been fermenting in her mind. If only she could persuade Aaron to allow her to use the place while the formalities over the proposed hotel were being decided by the government. Several possibilities had presented themselves to her almost immediately.

She smiled to herself. Before she had left the night before, she had arranged with Maria that they would meet in Leventos the following afternoon, once the girl had obtained the key from the owner. Karen wondered how Maria intended to persuade the old man to sell to a foreigner. Realising that that was not something she could influence, she put the problem out of her mind, content to leave that one to Maria.

Maria took a taxi to the small village in the mountains where Julio Escobar lived. He did not know she was coming, but Maria knew that wouldn't matter. It was time for her to visit again, and she knew that he would welcome her.

She felt a small dart of excitement deep in the pit of her belly. It wasn't easy to continue to be a 'good girl' now that she was fully grown. Tierra del Sol was a small, close-knit community, so playing around was not a viable option, not if she wanted to keep her reputation intact.

Maria smiled to herself as she thought of Karen's likely reaction to such an outdated concept as a woman's 'reputation'. But Karen lived in a different world, where different rules applied. Maria could marry, of course, as Ricardo wanted her to, but she knew in her heart she wasn't ready for that kind of restriction yet. Julio Escobar, her 'uncle' – the title was purely an honorary one, and indicative of the difference in their ages, as much as anything else – old as he was, was able to give her pleasure without breaking the sacred barrier of her maidenhood, and for that she was truly grateful.

Of course, this time she had an ulterior motive for visiting the old man. She wanted Karen to buy his bar, more than she had wanted anything for a long while.

Karen was wrong to assume it was because she wanted revenge, she told herself, as she climbed the steep hill which led to Escobar's *casa*. She actually wanted to *help* Ricardo, albeit in a round-about way. She wanted redemption for him, for she was convinced he would never find true happiness if he continued to live the way he had done for the past ten years.

It seemed like an omen that Karen had reappeared at this moment. Ricardo had loved her, even Maria's ten-year-old self had realised that. If only the time had been right for them, maybe her brother would not now be the dissolute individual he had become.

The bell to Escobar's *casa* resonated solemnly along the whitewashed corridors. The heavy, wooden door was opened by an elderly woman, dressed from head to toe in black, and with an expression to match.

'Good morning to you, Señora Ricas,' Maria said politely, avoiding the widow's disapproving eyes.

Dolores Ricas had worked as a live-in house-keeper and nurse to Escobar since her husband, Julio's brother, had died some twenty years before. Though she still clung to her widow's weeds, Maria knew that she hoped, one day, to marry Julio. Naturally, Señora Ricas did not welcome Maria's visits to the *casa*, though the girl knew she could rely on the widow's discretion, for the old man's sake, if not for her own.

Señora Ricas insisted on showing Maria through to Escobar's room, even though the girl knew the way by heart.

'Señorita Baddeiras,' she intoned gravely.

Julio Escobar turned towards the sound of her

103

voice, and Señora Ricas left, closing the door quietly, but firmly, behind her.

'Maria?'

'Yes, Uncle Julio, it is I.'

She went to kneel on the floor by his chair and he stroked her hair. At seventy, he was now completely blind, though his mind was as sharp as ever.

'How are you, Maria?'

'I am well, Uncle. How are you?'

The old man made a face.

'There are good days, and there are bad days. God decides. Today has become a good day with your arrival, and I thank Him for sending you to me. Would you like some refreshment? A cold lemonade, perhaps?'

Not wanting to see the old woman again, Maria shook her head.

'I am quite all right, thank you, Uncle.'

She laid her head in his lap and closed her eyes as he continued to stroke her hair. He always made her feel like a pampered pet, as if her skin was as soft as velvet under his fingers.

'Shall we pray together?' he said, after a few minutes.

'I should be most grateful for that,' she replied dutifully.

'Then I shall pray for the salvation of your soul, and for the Lord's guidance as to how I may help you to attain a state of heavenly bliss.'

He began to recite piously in Latin, the words made beautiful by the rich cadences of his voice. Maria closed her eyes. She was sure that she would never again be able to hear the beautiful prayer without becoming aroused, for this was how Escobar always began his seduction of her.

They sat in silence after he had finished. His fingertips traced light, sensitive circles on her neck and along her collarbones. Maria felt her breasts swell and her areolae draw into two small peaks as the slow, sensual warmth flooded through her. Escobar was so adept at seeking out her deepest, darkest desires, that he could arouse her with the slightest touch, the smallest word.

'Have you brought something for me?' he asked after a few minutes.

'Yes, of course.'

Maria reached into her bag and drew out a paper package. Inside were the panties she had worn the day before, unlaundered, which she passed to him.

The old man lifted the filmy scrap of fabric and brushed it lightly across his face. Then he scrunched it into a ball and inhaled deeply.

'Ah, the scent of nectar!' he breathed.

The first time he had done this, Maria had been mortified, embarrassed beyond measure. Now she felt only desire at his actions, and a perverse pleasure that he found the scent of her womanhood so pleasing.

'You are good to me, my child,' he said, finding the gusset of the panties and breathing deeply.

'Only, as you are to me,' she whispered, laying her hand on the soft bulge at his groin.

'Loosen your clothes, my dear, let me touch you,' he said.

Maria rose and unfastened her blouse. She never undressed fully for him, largely for fear that Señora

Ricas might come in and catch her. In any case, she found the state of *deshabillé* more arousing than total nudity, and her fingers trembled as she released the catch of the front-fastening bra she had worn deliberately for the occasion.

Reaching under her skirt, she removed her briefs, and passed this pair to Escobar to allow him to inhale their scent.

'So fresh!' he said, and his voice sounded like that of a young man.

Maria watched him sniffing at the scrap of lacy fabric, and knew that he would keep it, as a momento of the day, and to renew his pleasure for days to come. As she had expected, he pushed the panties into the pocket of his red quilted smoking jacket before gesturing for her to approach him.

'Come and sit on my knee,' he said, patting his lap.

Maria did so, aware that he was still strong enough to take her weight, despite his age. Looking into his face, she was still able to see the man he had been in his prime; hawkish, proud, not unlike Ricardo.

She smiled. Julio and her father had fallen out over a woman – Maria's mother, her father's second wife. Maria senior had, apparently, been betrothed to Julio, until she had fallen in love with his best friend, and married him instead. Though Julio and her father had never spoken after the marriage, Julio had still loved Maria's mother with a devotion that had never waned and, when her daughter had been born, he had transferred that love on to her. In her turn, Maria had always adored her 'Uncle' Julio.

'Ah! Your skin is as soft as holy milk,' he breathed, his hands caressing the contours of her upper body with gentle reverence. 'Such pretty young breasts – no one else has touched them have they Maria?' he asked her fiercely.

Maria winced as his hold on them tightened and she answered him quickly. 'No, Uncle, I am still pure.'

His grip loosened and he nodded, pleased with her response. 'You make an old man very happy, my dear. But one day you will marry, and then I shan't have the pleasure of your visits.'

'I will never abandon you,' she promised him, placing a gentle kiss on his wrinkled brow, 'you will always be very special to me.'

Her words caused Escobar to frown.

'You must not bring me such gifts when you are married, child, it would be against God's will. Still – ' he brightened and his sightless eyes crinkled attractively at the corners ' – that is for the future. Today we shan't concern ourselves with such unhappy thoughts!'

'No, Uncle,' Maria replied softly.

'What would you like me to do to bring you closer to the Lord, my child?'

The ritual was always the same – an evocation to the Almighty, and then a request for Maria to tell Julio how best he might serve her 'spiritual' development. She always gave the answers he expected, in a routine they had developed over the years of her maturity.

'I should like you to suck and kiss my breasts,' she said, making her voice small and deferential.

'Ah, yes – such wickedness!' he said, but already his hands were moving over Maria's generous globes, pinching and squeezing the tender flesh until he heard a gasp of pain.

'You might well gasp and cry, my child, but you must repent of your sins. Only pain will purge you of your unnatural desires.'

Dipping his head, he sought her nipple with his lips, lifting her breast to make it easier for himself. Maria moaned as the swollen teat was drawn into the heat of his mouth, and his teeth grazed the tender flesh.

'Oh, thank you,' she gasped as he drew deeply on its tip, sending spirals of pleasure through from her breast to her womb.

His fingers grasped at the other nipple and tweaked it savagely, causing her to cry out in shock. Pulling his head back roughly, he brought the fingers of his free hand up to the first nipple and twisted both, bringing tears to her eyes.

From past experience, Maria knew she just had to ride out the pain in order for it to slip surely, shockingly into the most intense pleasure. Escobar pulled her nipples away from her breasts as if testing their elasticity, stretching them to the point of agony before letting go and allowing them to spring back into shape.

Maria had never managed to reconcile the shame of being aroused by such abuse, and the next part of the ritual was the part she hated – and loved – the most.

'Have you learnt your lesson, my child?' the old man asked.

His voice was hoarse with suppressed desire and Maria knew he must curse the loss of his own physical abilities.

'Yes,' she replied demurely, knowing that her word alone would not be enough.

'Lift up your skirt.'

Maria did as he asked, aware that her vulva burned with shame.

'Open your legs, child, so that I may measure your virtue.'

Maria suffered his probing with a mixture of excitement and shame. She knew that her labia were slick with honey, the tender leaves of flesh swollen with desire. Escobar knew it too, yet he took his time, running his fingers along the channels before scooping up the moisture from the well of her vagina and lifting his fingertips to his nose.

He sniffed, like a gourmet chef testing the bouquet of a fine sauce.

'Ah!' he sighed, licking his fingers clean one by one. 'It saddens me, child, to tell you that your wickedness knows no bounds. Do you consent to being purged?'

'Yes, I do,' she said, hanging her head.

'Then you know what to do. Fetch me the box.'

Maria slipped off the old man's lap and went over to the bureau at the far side of the room. It was very old, brought into the family by Escobar's Andalusian great-grandmother in the previous century. The key was strapped to the underside of the bureau, and Maria felt for it with trembling fingers.

From the moment Escobar had introduced her to the dubious delights of the box, Maria had known that for her, sexual pleasure would never be as great as it was when spiked with a certain kind of pain. Escobar had divined her true nature and, though he shrouded their encounters in talk of the Almighty and the purging of her sin, Maria knew that these rituals were more to allay his own guilt: they had little to do with her.

Unlocking the bureau, she brought out the box, and carried it reverentially to Escobar.

'You know what to do,' he told her, when she reached him.

Maria placed the box carefully on the polished table at Escobar's side. It was heavy, made of intricately carved wood, lined with red velvet. Opening it, she shivered as she saw the contents of the lift-out wooden tray which formed the top section.

'Why do you hesitate, child?' Escobar asked, his voice low and kindly.

Maria stared at the perfectly crafted gold nipple clamps and her mouth went dry.

'I – I . . .'

'Pick up the clamps, Maria, and put them on.'

There was a cool authority in Escobar's voice which acted as a spur to her senses, making her quiver inside. Her fingers trembled as she picked up the first clamp. It was cold against her palm, and the cruel-looking, serrated edges, cunningly lined with fine, ancient red silk, gleamed at her.

'Good girl. Now, lean forward, let me touch you.'

Maria bent at the waist so that her breasts fell softly into the old man's hands.

'How big they are,' he murmured, his thumbs

110

passing back and forth across her nipples, making them tingle. 'It hurts me to have to punish you, Maria, but I hope you know I do it only for the good of your eternal soul.'

'Yes,' she whispered, by now used to his hypocrisy and not minding about it at all.

It was worse, somehow, having to attach the clamps to her nipples herself. If Escobar had performed the deed, it would not have felt quite so . . . depraved. She wanted to be able to pretend that the pain was being inflicted upon her against her will. But Escobar was very clever – he knew that her ultimate submission, her ultimate bliss, would come from the unbearable shame of showing herself to be eager for this.

Escobar was stroking one breast, running his palms along its slopes so that it elongated between them, forcing the tumescent nipple to stand out even more prominently. Maria opened the clamp and, positioning its open maw around the nub of flesh, she let it go. Despite the fact that she was prepared for the sharp shock of pain she still cried out, tears running freely down her face until it subsided to a dull, strangely pleasurable throb.

The second nipple was just as sensitive, shrinking from the teeth of the clamp as she positioned it. Escobar pulled on it, as if milking her, until once again it found a long pink tube of flesh, so that when Maria let the spring go, it caught her mercilessly, making her cry afresh.

Escobar loved her to cry. He said it was a sign from God that her sins were being purged, but Maria knew it was merely that the thought of her tears gave him a sense of power over her which, in his frail state of health, he did not often feel in life any more.

He reached for her now and licked at her face, catching her tears on his tongue. 'There, there, little one,' he crooned, his fingers stroking her breasts softly and gently, 'do not cry. Save your tears for later.'

'I am sorry, truly I am,' she whispered.

Escobar patted her cheek with a tenderness which brought fresh tears to her eyes. 'Pass me my cane,' he said, his voice brisk now, belying his age.

There was a selection of walking sticks in the umbrella stand by the door. Amongst them, Maria knew, was a short, thin, whippy little cane in pale wood which Escobar kept there expressly for this purpose. Her hand trembled as she brought it to him.

'Kiss the instrument of your salvation,' he told her.

Maria touched her lips to the cruel length of the cane before handing it to him. Escobar slashed the air, then nodded once.

'Bend from the waist, my dear. Can you feel the clamps pulling on your wicked teats?'

'Yes,' Maria gasped, as her breasts were pulled downward by the heavy gold clips attached to them.

She gasped again as he reached out and gave each of them a twist, increasing her discomfort. Then the cane swished softly through the air and struck her on the upper slope of her breasts.

'Oh! God help me!' she cried, as the stinging

sensation seared through her, taking her breath away.

'That's right, child. Pray to the Lord!'

This time the cane landed on the undersides of her breasts, making them jiggle and shake and fill with a searing heat.

Maria knew he would not hit her again – this was enough to send a desire so strong it hurt her through to her womb. She took the cane from Escobar without comment, and went to put it back in the umbrella stand.

'May I please take off the clamps now?' she asked him, knowing already what the answer would be.

'All in good time,' child,' he said, as she had known he would. 'Let me see if your punishment has dried the fount of your wickedness.'

Maria stood obediently in front of him, her legs apart. The faint stripes on her breasts were stinging and her nipples ached under the clamps. Escobar insinuated his forefinger between her labia. It slipped easily through her folds, aided by the copious juices produced at the core of her sex.

'Ah, I fear your wickedness knows no bounds!' he said, only this time he was unable to mask the delight in his voice as he spoke. 'Fetch me the balls.'

Maria lifted the wooden tray which had held the nipple clamps to reveal the two gold balls, connected by a fine chain, nestling in a bed of red velvet. As she picked them up, they weighed heavily against her palm, and a pulse began to beat deep inside her sex.

The Chinese love-balls were ancient, polished to a dull shine by the feminine juices of countless concubines over the centuries. They clacked dully together as she passed them to Escobar.

The old man rolled them in his hands, caressing their surface with his fingertips, as if reacquainting himself with an old and familiar friend.

'Come closer, child,' he said, beckoning to her.

Maria stood in front of him her eyes glazed, unable to think of anything now but the delicious humiliation to come.

'Bend your legs.'

The precious metal had taken on some of the heat of Escobar's skin, so the balls were warm as he rolled them against her inner thigh. Maria concentrated on breathing deeply, in and out, in and out, knowing that it was vital for her to relax if Escobar was to be able to insert them without breaking her stretched hymen.

He had done it twice before, each time being careful not to damage the physical evidence of her virginity in order to protect her honour. He swore he could still feel the maiden barrier, as her husband would be able to on her wedding night.

Now he eased the golden balls inside her, pressing them home with his forefinger. The balls filled her, stretching the sides of her feminine passage. When she moved, they rolled together with a muffled clicking noise which clearly delighted Escobar.

'Beautiful, beautiful!' he breathed, his lips curving into a smile of pure pleasure. 'How I wish I could see you! Tell me how you look, Maria – describe to me what I would see if I were not blind.'

Maria knew that this was part of her humiliation, and yet she could find nothing in her to rebel

114

against his edict. Rather, she revelled in the opportunity to debase herself, even while she was being assailed by a potent rush of shame.

'My – my breasts are swollen, the nipples are pulled downward by the clamps.'

'Are they sore?'

'Oh, yes, they are so sore,' she said, unable to hold back a small sob. 'Please may I release them?'

'In a moment,' he said, clearly relishing her sexual distress. 'Tell me what else I would be able to see.'

'You would see that I am standing with my legs apart, and that my – my sex bulges with its burden – oh, the clamps – please . . .!'

'Very well. If it pleases God, you may remove the clamps.'

Maria braced herself for the short, sharp pain which always accompanied her release, and let out a small gasp of momentary distress. Escobar reached for her, and drew each abused nipple into his mouth in turn. Soothing it with his lips and tongue, he set up a chain reaction throughout Maria's body which sent a fresh rush of moisture to her sex. She groaned softly and stroked the top of his head. She was filled with gratitude towards him, for at that moment she felt truly alive.

'Is that better, little one?' he asked, when he had finished.

'Yes, thank you,' she replied, rubbing her burning areolae with her palms.

'Then let us continue the punishment,' he said.

Maria found the small, flat leather paddle which he kept in the bureau, and fell to her knees to one side of him. At his signal, she leant across his lap, presenting her exposed buttocks to him.

Escobar began to pray again, as if hoping for inspiration from the Almighty. Then he beat her.

The paddle stung her flesh, but Maria barely noticed this new discomfort. Instead, she was aware of the gold balls rolling wildly inside her, and of her sex lips swelling and moistening as her body rocked back and forth.

Past discretion, she thrust her hand down between her legs and, as Escobar continued to slap her flesh buttocks, she rubbed furiously at her clitoris, bringing herself to an orgasm so intense that she rose up on to her knees, knocking Escobar's hand away. The gold balls fell out of her body and on to the thick carpet with a soft 'plop' as her sex convulsed.

The old man listened to her moaning and sobbing with a look of beatific satisfaction on his aged face, and Maria knew that through her, he had himself come as close to ecstasy as he ever could. Then it was over.

Neither Maria nor Escobar spoke as she readjusted her clothing and put all the instruments of her 'salvation' away in the box. He waited until he heard her lock it away in the bureau before saying, quite conversationally, 'I'll ask Señora Rica for that lemonade now, shall I?'

Maria smiled affectionately at him. 'That would be wonderful, Uncle Julio,' she replied, taking a seat on the sofa opposite.

By the time Señora Rica arrived, Maria was every inch the respectful honorary niece, paying her aged uncle a dutiful visit. Maria had to hide a smile as the old woman peered suspiciously at her before going to fetch them lemonade and cake. What would she say if she knew that the girl was sitting without her briefs, which were, even now, nestling in her uncle's jacket pocket?

When she had gone, Escobar asked, 'Is there anything I can do for you, my dear, any small favour I can help you with?'

Normally, Maria always declined, so he raised his eyebrows in mild surprise when this time she said, 'Actually, Uncle, there is something.'

'Really?' You have only to ask, child, you know that.'

'It is about the old bar in Leventos. I have a friend who would like to buy it. If it pleases you to please me, Uncle, I want you to consider their offer.'

Escobar's face clouded and she saw the anger playing around his lips.

'Did that rogue, Ricardo send you to ask this?'

'No, most definitely not. The person who wants to buy this bar is a foreigner. Wait – please hear me out,' she said, as Escobar began to splutter indignantly. 'I know you would want to sell to a foreigner even less than you would want to sell to Ricardo, but I think you might be interested in the plans we have for the bar.'

Escobar listened intently. When he heard how Maria and Karen intended to make life difficult for Ricardo, he roared with laughter.

'We will have our lemonade, child, then we will talk some more.'

117

Maria sat patiently while they took the refreshment grudgingly offered by Señora Ricas, knowing that it was no use rushing the old man into a decision. When at last the lemonade and cake had been cleared away, he sat back in his seat and turned his sightless eyes towards her.

'I will let you have this bar, my child, but only if you allow me to take the foreign purchaser's money and put it into an account for you.'

'Uncle?'

'I have long wanted to give you some money of your own, my child, and I feel this could be the answer, especially as it seems that you will retain some interest in the property. I think it better if we use this clandestine approach, don't you, my child? Lest your brother should find out you are a woman of independent means, and wonder at its source.'

Maria considered for a moment, then she went over to kiss the old man's dry cheek.

'Thank you, Uncle Julio,' she said quietly. 'By giving me the means to an independent life, you have given me a gift beyond price.'

Escobar's hand patted her cheek, and she swore she saw tears gathering in the corners of his useless eyes.

'That is no more than you have given me, my child.'

He smiled at her as she left him, and Maria knew that he would not expect her to visit him again. Her sadness at the thought was momentary, however, for before her she had the prospect of a new life – and Karen, though she did not yet know it, was going to be instrumental in its realisation.

Chapter Six

*A*aron had taken some persuading to agree to Karen's plan. It was only the promise of a share in the girls' profits that had swayed him, eventually, into agreeing that they could use the property for whichever purpose they chose until the necessary permits to build the hotel he wanted on the site were obtained. The sale went through with a speed that took Karen's breath away and so, after only one month as Wingspan's replacement rep, she resigned her post to concentrate on her new venture.

Maria and Karen celebrated with a bottle of wine in the dusty main room of what had formerly been Escobar's bar.

'I can't wait to see Ricardo's face when he finds out who has beaten him to the purchase of Uncle Julio's bar!' Maria said, stifling a giggle.

Karen's eyes flashed, but she kept her thoughts

private. *She* couldn't wait to see Ricardo's face when she started to lure away, first his customers, then his staff.

'When can we start work on the conversion?' she asked, keeping the conversation on a business level.

'Right away. My uncle has put a team of workmen at our disposal, but really it is more a case of cleaning and decorating, don't you think?'

Karen looked around her. The property consisted of a large, rectangular room, with an L-shaped counter running parallel to the entire length of one of the shorter walls and half of one of the adjacent longer ones. Narrowing her eyes, she imagined the dusty floorboards sanded and stained, the bar polished and stocked, and the torn and dusty curtains replaced by bright, modern blinds.

'We should keep it bright, no?' Maria said. 'And comfortable, to attract the ladies?'

Karen nodded. 'How about sofas and little slipper chairs around glass-topped tables? And if we knock through and gut the kitchen, we could build a small stage at the end of the room.'

'Yes! And the cloakrooms – could we make them look like boudoirs?'

'Yes, it doesn't have to be too expensive. We could use lots of large, green plants, and provide complimentary cosmetics and toiletries.'

Maria grinned. 'In Ricardo's bar, the ladies' toilets are disgusting. I am so excited, Karen; we could make this bar into a place where *we* would like to spend our time!'

Karen smiled at her. Maria's excitement was infectious, but she wondered whether this was the right time to reveal her own, hidden agenda. She decided to proceed with caution.

'I should like the use of the large room at the back, Maria, for my own, private purposes.'

Maria must, however, have picked up on something in her tone, for she raised her eyebrows. 'There are four rooms upstairs, too. Do you have plans for them all?'

'Would you like a room of your own?'

'I would like one to be set aside as a dressing room, for all the performers who will come to entertain our guests.'

Karen nodded. 'That's a good idea. And the other three?'

Maria gave her one of her unnervingly perceptive looks. 'I have a feeling that you have plans for those,' she said.

Karen smiled. 'What would you think, Maria, if I proposed that we model our bar on the Bar del Amore, but with a twist?'

Maria regarded her warily. 'Go on.'

'Consider for a moment – why do women flock to your brother's bar, Maria?'

Maria shrugged, and Karen could tell that she was trying to guess the direction the conversation was taking.

'I don't know. To drink, to listen to music . . . for romance – poor fools!'

'Exactly! They go looking for romance, and end up having a one-night stand, then getting dumped. But what if there was somewhere they could enjoy sex on their own terms?'

'I don't understand.'

Karen made a sweeping gesture with her arm. 'Supposing we were to employ clean, attentive, attractive young men to provide sex on tap at our bar?'

'You mean ... you want to run a brothel, for women?'

Karen laughed gently at Maria's unfettered outrage.

'Not a brothel, Maria – I'm not proposing that we turn into a couple of madams. Does Ricardo charge his customers for sex? Of course not. He employs his bar studs to entice the girls in, and probably gets away with paying them peanuts, too, in exchange for ripe pickings. Am I right?'

Maria shrugged and rolled her eyes. 'Probably. So, how would we pay our ... boys, Karen?'

Karen looked at her with a glint in her eye that made Maria suck in her breath.

'We wouldn't have to *pay* them, Maria. We'll employ only those who are willing to serve in return for their bed and board.'

Angels opened six weeks later, to a flurry of publicity on the island. Karen and Maria had spent hours handing out flyers to the numerous hotels and apartment buildings, explaining to all the reps how Angels was to be a women-only retreat, where everything would be provided for their pleasure.

Karen flew over two of her past conquests, Dale and Peter, from England, offering them a free two-week holiday if they would act as her 'bar boys' until she was able to recruit some local talent.

Standing with Maria on the opening night, watching the three dozen or so curious women who had responded to their general invitation, Karen knew it was time to start work in earnest.

Ricardo stood outside the Bar del Amore with a cigarillo between his fingers, and watched the activity across the street. It was a nine-day wonder, of course, this bar that said it was run by women, for women, but he resented even one night's loss of business.

Maria's betrayal still burned brightly in his heart, but not even that could mask his anger towards Karen. He had thought that when he saw her again – No! he would not allow any tender thoughts to pass through his head! She had used him that first night, then tossed him aside like a broken toy. All of his attempts to see or to speak to her had come to nothing, and the humiliation of her lack of interest in him still rankled.

She had been busy insofar as his bar was concerned, though – oh yes! Karen had made sure that Ricardo had received visits from a stream of government agencies, from public health inspectors to the fire department, and the sudden flurry of official interest in the Bar del Amore had been reported widely in the local press, even reaching the mainland papers. Consequently, there had been a significant drop in door numbers over the past few weeks, and the takings were down to a worrying level.

But this – opening a bar in direct competition to his – was the last straw. On top of the problems Karen had made for him since she had arrived, this could be enough to send him out of business. It was clear that she wanted to hound him, but she had gone too far this time.

'What do you think they plan to do over there?'

Ricardo turned as Darren joined him and scowled. 'Who ever understands a woman's motive?' he asked bitterly.

Darren shrugged his shoulders. 'It's virtually empty in there,' he said, stabbing his thumb back towards the bar. 'Whatever they've got, it's cleared us out for the night.'

'Novelty value,' Ricardo said, throwing his half-finished cigarillo down on the ground. 'That's all it is. Give the boys a few hours' break – tell them to be back by eleven – we might start to get a bit busier then.'

He went back inside, seething inwardly. Darren stopped him at the doorway.

'Do you think we ought to go over, see what's going on?' he suggested.

'Women only, isn't it? The only men in there are the ones employed to serve behind the bar.'

'Then maybe one of us should apply for a job?'

'Don't be a fool, Maria knows every one of you!'

'Yeah. Sorry, Ric, I wasn't thinking . . .' His voice faded as he saw that his boss was frowning deeply.

'Unless – we've got a couple of new recruits arriving at the end of the week, haven't we?' mused Ricardo.

'Uh huh. They're both due on Saturday.'

'I wonder . . . Keep them out of sight when they arrive, Darren. Maybe we could use one of them to infiltrate the opposition.

The two men grinned at each other, happier now that they felt they might be able to do something positive.

'Oh, I almost forgot. I came to tell you there's someone to see you in the bar. A bird.'

Ricardo raised his eyebrows. He wasn't expecting anyone. In fact, since the debacle with Karen, he hadn't felt the need for a woman at all. It had worried him, though he told himself repeatedly that it did not mean their encounter had rekindled any deep feelings he may have had for her. On the contrary, it must be that Karen's behaviour had simply put him off all women for the time being. But it also meant that there was no tourist currently on the island who might come looking for him, and he was puzzled.

He walked into the bar to look for the woman who was waiting for him. She was sitting on a bar stool, fidgeting nervously with the hem of her skirt, which had ridden up to expose one of her plump, pink thighs. She looked vaguely familiar and, as she turned her head, Ricardo felt a jolt of recognition. If only he could remember her name . . .

'Hello, Ricardo,' she said, her voice soft and tremulous, as if she wasn't sure of the reception she might receive.

'Darling,' he said, smiling blandly at her. 'What brings you here?'

The girl fiddled with the ends of her hair, tucking one blonde strand up behind her ear.

'I – I had a lot of annual leave building up, so I decided to book myself another two weeks in Leventos. It seems extravagant, I know,' she said,

125

with a nervous giggle, 'and it is terribly self-indulgent, but ... I couldn't get you out of my mind, Ricardo, and I kept thinking – maybe if it hadn't been my last day that day we met, if we'd had more time to get to know each other – well ...'

She raised her hands in a small gesture of helplessness. Ricardo arranged his features carefully, so that they would not betray his mounting dismay.

'But – surely you have not spent all this money on another holiday just to see me?' he said.

The girl's face fell, and the way she avoided his eyes as she replied told him all he needed to know.

'Of course not! This is such a beautiful island: I had such a good time here ...'

'Weren't you with friends before?' he asked her, his memory of her gradually returning.

'That's right. But this time I'm all alone.'

Ricardo felt a twinge of compassion for her. He remembered her now: her name was Anita and they had spent an afternoon together some six or seven weeks before. The poor girl must be very unhappy if she had pinned her hopes on such a flimsy relationship.

'Anita, I don't know what to say.'

'Say you're glad I'm here,' she said, fervently. 'Say you're pleased to see me.'

Ricardo gazed into her warm, sherry-brown eyes, which were looking at him with such a fierce need, and knew he should let her down now, gently, but very firmly. Regardless of what she might have imagined had passed between them during that solitary afternoon, to Ricardo it had been no more than a physical encounter. Pleasant at the time, but, ultimately, quite forgettable.

In truth, he didn't remember too much about her. He recalled thinking she wasn't too bright, and her behaviour in chasing back to Leventos after him on the strength of a one night stand confirmed his guess. He also remembered that the sex had been pretty good, and suddenly he felt the lack of it in his life the past few weeks. After all, she was virtually offering herself to him on a plate, with all the trimmings – for the love of all that is holy, he thought, he was a red-blooded man, not a saint!

Of course, he would have to disillusion her – eventually. Right now, all he could see was the moist softness of her lips as they parted winsomely, and his cock took over from his brain.

'I *am* glad you are here. And I am *very* pleased to see you. Shall we go upstairs?'

The tension slipped from Anita's face as she searched his eyes and decided he was sincere. He held out his hand and helped her down from the bar stool before letting her walk before him up the back stairs.

This time, he hadn't had the chance to ask Darren to clear up and make the room ready. The bed was crumpled and unmade and the chart on the wall, its list of names substantially added to over the past six weeks by the boys who worked for him, was displayed in a prominent position.

Anita didn't seem to notice. She appeared to be so grateful that Ricardo hadn't rejected her outright, that she was through the outer room and into the bedroom before he could catch up with her.

Her eagerness transmitted itself to Ricardo, and he found himself hardening at the sight of her removing her clothes. Her skin was white and soft, with no trace of the light tan she had acquired on her last visit to Tierra del Sol. Ricardo didn't remember her being quite so plump, and he guessed that she had gained weight since returning home.

'I never forgot you,' she said, throwing her lingerie aside and standing naked before him.

Ricardo's eyes ran languidly over her generous figure, lingering on the cushiony swell of her breasts, and the soft, downy fluff on her mons. He could see her trembling from the other side of the room, and guessed that she had worked herself up into such a state through anticipating this meeting.

The thought that this girl had flown miles from home to sleep with him, and that, by her own admission, she had fantasised and dreamt about him for six weeks, gave him the firmest erection he had had for a long time. He knew then that he was going to enjoy this.

'Nor I you, my darling,' he lied softly. 'Come and feel how well I remember you.'

Anita moved slowly across the room, her eyes never leaving his as she approached him. She smelt of floral perfume, fresh perspiration, and the heavy, yeasty scent of feminine arousal. Reaching for her, Ricardo closed his eyes and allowed himself to be transported away from the irritations of the night, and into a state of bliss.

* * *

Karen stood in the shadows where she was least conspicuous, and watched as Angels came to life. Their vigorous advertising campaign had obviously captured the collective female imagination, for the place was jammed solid. Even now, Peter was having to turn disappointed would-be patrons away at the door, but not before he'd given each of them a half-price voucher for the following evening to soften the blow.

She could see Maria happily helping out behind the bar, her lovely face flushed with excitement. Across the room, Dale was coping manfully with the demands of a group of women who were obviously the worse for drink, and she made a mental note to reward him later.

For Karen, persuading both Dale and Peter to join her for this initial period had been something of a coup. Both had high-powered, demanding jobs and neither could really afford the time, but here they were, so eager to do her a favour that they had rejigged schedules and cancelled contracts, and all for the chance of spending two weeks near her.

Karen smiled to herself, pleased to see the results of her training. Although it had been more than a year since she had last seen Dale, he still kept his body depilated and smooth, as she had instructed him to and, still piercing his navel was a ring she had given him, to which was connected a fine chain which passed through another piercing in his left nipple.

He also remembered everything she had taught him about pleasing a woman, too. Two days earlier, after he had settled into the small room he was to share with Peter, Karen had wasted no time in summoning him to the large room, leading off from the main bar, which she had appropriated.

Dale had gaped in amazement at the matt black paint on the walls and the specially installed furniture she had had flown over from Madrid.

'Wow,' he had said. 'This is unbelievable!'

'But exciting, yes?' Karen had said, emerging from the carefully positioned shadows so that he saw her fully for the first time.

'Very exciting,' he had agreed, though his eyes had been not on her custom-built dungeon, but on Karen herself, resplendent in shiny black PVC.

She had chosen to wear a short, black, tabard-style dress, teamed with stiff, PVC gauntlets which reached the middle of her upper arm, and the thigh-high boots with spiky, six-inch heels which she knew would turn him on instantly. There was little time for subtle games, and she wanted him in place, both physically and psychologically, before the bar opened.

Dale had gazed at her and, instantly, his erection had strained against the front of his cool cotton chinos.

'I see you haven't forgotten me,' she said, casting a glance at the tell-tale bulge. 'Have you remembered everything else?'

'Oh, *everything*, Karen,' he said fervently. 'How could I ever forget?'

Karen had walked up to him, a rush of affection softening her tone as she greeted him.

'It's lovely to see you, darling,' she whispered, against the silky softness of his long black hair.

'Now, take off your clothes for me, so that I can have a look at you.'

Holding her eye he had obliged, peeling off his shirt and trousers to reveal his nakedness beneath.

'No underwear?'

'You warned me not to wear any, Karen, in case you should ever send for me unexpectedly.'

His words sent a dart of desire through her, so potent it made her shiver. The thought of this smooth young City futures salesman sitting at his desk all day hoping for her call, his naked cock in direct contact with his sober city suit, satisfied her sense of propriety, and the fact that he still wore the chain and ring through his piercings was an added thrill. Karen was touched.

'You still wear my mark close to your heart, I see,' she said softly, placing her hand over it.

'Always,' he said, his voice gruff with emotion and dutifully suppressed desire.

Karen ran her fingertips across his smooth, oiled skin, checking for any sign of body hair. She found none, and it thrilled her anew to think that he continued to submit himself to his monthly visits to the beauty salon where he endured the painful waxing which kept him smooth and hair-free.

Then she had stepped back, distancing herself. It was time to go to work on him.

'So, Dale, what makes a healthy, red-blooded 23-year-old man debase himself daily in the forlorn hope that his mistress might call?'

'It was a hope that was realised, in the end,' he said earnestly. 'You *did* call for me, eventually.'

Karen had smiled slowly. 'Indeed I did. For a

very special purpose. First, though,' she said briskly, moving away from him, 'you must prove to me that you have remembered *everything* I have taught you.'

She noted the eagerness in his eyes and hid a smile. Dale was one of the few of her lovers who submitted to her demands out of a genuine desire to please her. She suspected that he didn't actually like punishment very much, and so he didn't deliberately disobey her in the hope that she might be provoked into picking up her whip, or chastising him in some other way, as did so many. For Dale, Karen's contempt, her displeasure, was enough to cast him into the depths of despondency for hours, and her pleasure and approval were the only things that could lift him back out again. Over Dale she had a power which went beyond the physical, and transcended time and distance.

'What a lovely, responsive cock,' she purred, taking it into her hand and stroking its velvety tip with her thumb. 'Is this meant for me?'

Dale's Adam's apple bobbed as he swallowed. 'If it pleases you, Karen,' he whispered hoarsely.

Karen made a show of thinking about it, before shaking her head. 'I think not. Perhaps when you've earned it, in a fortnight – but only if you're very, very good.'

She pinched the end, trapping the sap she could feel rising and Dale let out a small, involuntary groan.

'I have something for you,' she said.

She led him by the prick across the room, then opened one of the cupboards there and took out a leather sheath. A look of dismay passed across Dale's eyes, but was swiftly extinguished, as she had taught him.

Karen handed him the sheath and watched as he slipped it over his straining cock. When it was fitted, she took the straps and fastened one around his thigh, binding his tumescent cock firmly, and uncomfortably, against it.

'Karen –'

'Ssh!' She touched her fingertips against his taut lips. 'Remember that for you, before pleasure, there must always be pain. It is better, that way. Here, this is something you might enjoy . . .'

She pulled her skirt up slowly to reveal her naked mons. Dale's eyes widened as she leant against the end of one of two metal couches set in the middle of the room and pushed her feet further apart.

Karen knew that she was wet, that the mere proximity of him had served to arouse her, had made her want at least a part of him. There was a wonderful energy about him, a vitality that cut through social convention and tapped into the very essence of life. It was what had attracted her to him in the first place. It was what made her dominion over him so pleasing, so valuable to her, and why it gave her so much satisfaction.

Seeing his cue, Dale dropped to his knees in front of her. The joyful light in his eyes at her decision to let him serve her chased away the disappointment he had felt when she had handed him the cock restraint.

Placing her hands on the cold stainless steel, Karen hoisted herself up, so that she was sitting on the end of the hard couch. Dale's face was now level with her groin, and he could barely wait for her signal before he touched her.

'No hands,' she had said softly. 'Make me come with your mouth.'

And he had done. Needing no further urging, Dale had clasped his hands behind his back and parted Karen's swollen labia carefully with his lips and tongue. His long, silky black hair brushed against the sensitive flesh of her inner thighs, making her gasp with pleasure.

He was a master of cunnilingus. Kissing her open sex-lips as he might have kissed her mouth, he coaxed her clitoris from beneath its hood with the tip of his tongue. Instinctively, he seemed to know exactly how much pressure to apply as he teased the hardening bud with tiny, flicking caresses before running his tongue languidly along the heated channels of flesh on either side of it.

Karen had closed her eyes and leant back on her elbows, content to take her pleasure from him as he worked at her tender flesh, drawing the sweetness from her before plundering the gateway to her body with the very tip of his tongue.

She had come in a series of warm, rolling waves, scissoring her legs around Dale's head and holding him close to her as her sex convulsed and gave up its pleasure. As soon as her climax began to subside, though, she pushed him gently away, with her spike heels braced against his shoulders, and he sat back on his haunches.

'That was lovely, darling,' she had purred, running

her long, gloved fingers over his chest. 'Are you very uncomfortable?'

Glancing at his leather-covered penis, Karen had seen that it had swollen to monstrous proportions and that the glossy hide sheath was straining to contain it. The end of the pouch was damp with the leakage from his cock-tip, but he was prevented from gaining any real satisfaction by the constriction of his bondage.

'I am a little,' he had admitted meekly.

Karen had smiled cruelly.

'Poor love,' she had crooned. 'Still, if you continue to give me pleasure, you will get your just reward in the end. You may go back to your room now, Dale.'

Dale had turned obediently and, still wearing the leather pouch, had left her. He was wearing it even now, as he endured the attention of the women who flocked around him, and Karen knew that, though he would be uncomfortable, he would relish the discomfort. He knew she would reward him for his fortitude, eventually. And for the privilege of making love fully to Karen, he would endure far, far worse, if necessary.

From the way he was being shamelessly exploited by the women, Karen guessed that it might indeed be very necessary and she smiled.

Ricardo stood very still as Anita unbuttoned his shirt and eased it off over his shoulders. Close to, the smell of her perfume overwhelmed all the other aromas he had detected when she had first approached him. It was heavy and cloying and, combined with the miasma of stale cigarette smoke and the ever-present scent of sex in the room, it made him feel faintly nauseous.

Anita's lips moved across his skin, clinging and demanding, and after a few moments he felt he would be consumed by her if he did not move. Yet something kept him immobile; something made him stand passively as she pushed his trousers and shorts down over the hard length of his thighs to his ankles.

Kicking his clothing clear, Ricardo moved to sit on the bed, shifting back so that he was leaning against the headboard, with an uninterrupted view of Anita's naked body moving above his. She bent forward and her fleshy breasts hung down, swinging freely as she moved, and he reached up to touch them.

Her pink-lipsticked lips felt full and soft as she opened them around the tip of his cock. Ricardo sighed and made himself more comfortable as his body reacted to the heat of her mouth and the delicious drawing sensation induced by her sucking.

He needed this. Closing his eyes, he imagined it was Karen leaning over him, her mouth full of his cock, and he tilted up his hips, thrusting deeper into the girl's mouth. He would like to get Karen in this position, to stamp on her his authority, his possession of her.

Anita moaned as he reached behind her neck and pulled her face down, on to his groin. He could feel her throat contracting wildly as she tried to take him, and he had to pull back to give her a chance to catch her breath.

He allowed her only a moment's respite before thrusting back in, filling her mouth, using it as he would her sex.

Anita sensed the change in him and tried, instinctively to pull away, but Ricardo, anticipating her move, held fast on to the back of her neck. She couldn't speak, but she struggled for a moment before realising it was hopeless.

Ricardo felt the fight go out of her, and sensed the moment when she realised she didn't actually want him to stop, after all. Her entire body seemed to soften and melt, and her eyes closed in an expression of bliss. He felt the rhythm of her sucking change and knew that she was enjoying it for its own sake now, not just doing it because she thought it was what he wanted.

This new perspective excited him, and he felt the ejaculate pooling in the base of his cock.

'Swallow it,' he murmured as the first hot jets burst out of him. 'Drink it all down . . .'

Anita struggled, but managed to do as he instructed, swallowing his semen as it poured from him whilst still attempting to milk him with her lips. As he came, he recalled how good the sex had been before, and how empty it had left him feeling. *Not this time*, he vowed. This time he was going to make the most of every minute of the encounter and leave the soul-searching for later, if it had to come at all.

As soon as he was spent, he pulled out of Anita's mouth and regarded her thoughtfully. Her white skin was pink and flushed and there was a brightness to her eyes that hadn't been there earlier.

'Do you remember me now?' she asked him breathlessly.

'Did you doubt it before?'

Her eyes clouded slightly, but she smiled as she nodded.

Ricardo allowed his own eyes to roam appreciatively over her naked body as she knelt beside him on the bed. He recalled that the last time he had taken her from behind after spanking her luscious bottom, but he had no inclination to indulge in that kind of game today.

Anita gave an excited little squeal and he followed her gaze to where his cock was beginning to stand proud again from the nest of coarse black hair at his groin. Smiling, he drew her into his arms and lifted himself up, so that he was looking down at her.

Slipping his hand between her legs, he probed the sticky folds of her sex, searching for the swollen nub of her clitoris amidst the slippery lips. It quivered momentarily and then a strong pulse began to beat against his fingerpads.

'Lovely girl,' he whispered, moving his fingers rhythmically across the eager flesh, 'so wet and ready. What would you like to do now?'

Anita moaned softly, her eyes closing as his touch worked its magic.

'Make me come, Ricardo,' she murmured. 'Please . . . let me feel it coming . . .'

Ricardo watched her face as he manipulated her tender nub, gauging exactly when to increase the pressure, or slow his rhythm. He knew it was possible to keep her teetering on the brink for hours, if he wanted to, but his purpose tonight was more prosaic. He wanted her to be hot and wet and willing to permit him any liberty before he himself came again.

Judging that the time was right, he rubbed harder at the tiny bundle of nerve endings which held the key to her submission.

'Oh – oh yes, I'm coming now . . . I'm coming . . . *I'm coming!*' she shouted, sitting upright and grasping at his shoulders as the feelings overwhelmed her.

Ricardo wasted no time in pushing her down again, on to her back, and positioning himself between her outspread thighs. Taking advantage of the last tremors of her climax, he moved inside the hot, slippery well of her sex, feeling her vaginal walls enclose him, and draw him further into her with every fading convulsion.

To be inside her was blissful, and Ricardo wished for nothing more at that moment than to simply rest inside her body before beginning to move slowly in and out of her. Anita, however, had other ideas. Bringing her legs up and around his waist, she placed her heels against the dip in the small of his back and pulled him deeper into her.

Subject to his own physical responses, Ricardo felt the sensations begin to build, too soon, too quickly. Angry at her for precipitating his climax, he thrust savagely into her, feeling her whole body shake with each inward stroke.

To his surprise, Anita meshed her fingers into his

hair and pulled it viciously. Silently, like combatants, they rolled off the bed and on to the floor. Pinning her to the ground with his upper body, Ricardo subjugated her in the only way he could think of: by taking her hard and fast, pistoning his cock in and out of her as she had longed for him to do.

Anita cried out, uttering a stream of incoherent nonsense-words as she felt him come, his cock pulsing strongly, deep inside her vagina. As soon as he was finished, Ricardo pulled out of her and rolled on to his back. Staring up at the ceiling, he realised they were both panting, both breathless, and that their breathing sounded harsh in the confines of the bedroom.

After a few minutes, Anita's hand crept tentatively into his. He didn't withdraw his hand, but neither did he make any attempt to hold hers, and after a few minutes she moved it away again.

As if by unspoken agreement, they rose and picked up their discarded clothes. Now that he had enjoyed her, Ricardo could barely bring himself to look at her. He wondered how he could let her down without causing her too much distress, but failed to come up with any answers.

He needn't have bothered. As Anita walked out of the bedroom and into the outer room, she caught sight of the 'shagometer' hanging on the wall.

'What's this?' she said, peering myopically at it.

'It's nothing,' he replied, trying to steer her towards the stairs.

But Anita had caught sight of her own name on the chart, coupled with those of Ricardo and Jamie.

Moving her eyes along to her 'rating', she saw that, in amongst the 'juicy peaches' and 'virgin holes', she had been designated a 'willing pig'.

Ricardo cringed as she turned on him.

'You bastard! How could you?' she asked, her voice horribly small.

'Anita – '

'I trusted you. Oh, I know I was foolish to come back chasing after a dream that I see now never really existed, but I thought at least that you were a decent human being. What are you going to write on your chart now, Ricardo? That the pig kept coming back for more?'

'Please, Anita – '

'Fuck off, Ricardo.'

'Don't leave like this, I – '

'And just for the record, you're not exactly a "juicy peach" yourself – I faked it!' she cried, as she ran down the stairs and out into the night.

Ricardo swore violently and ripped the chart from the wall. What had started out as a bit of lighthearted fun amongst the boys had turned into something destructive and dishonourable. He heard the lower door slam as Anita left, and he felt a jolt of remorse. He had used her, sure, but he hadn't intended for her to feel this humiliation. She didn't deserve it, and it made him feel bad. At that moment, he didn't like himself very much, and this unwelcome feeling stayed with him as he went back downstairs.

Anita ran out into the darkened street without any clear idea of where she was going. She had only thought to get out, to get away from him. Knowing that she had made an outsized fool of herself made her feel sick and she didn't know how she was going to hold her head high in the morning. Now, though, all she wanted was to find somewhere to lick her wounds.

Unlike the Bar del Amore, the bar opposite was buzzing with activity, so she ran around to the back of the building, where she knew there would be shadows. Just as she rounded the corner, a beautiful, dark-haired girl was taking out a bag of rubbish, and Anita ran, literally, right into her arms.

'My God! What is it? Has someone hurt you?' the girl asked, drawing her into the light.

Careless of the way she knew she must look, wild-eyed and dishevelled, Anita clung to the girl, sensing in her the potential for friendship.

'Yes! she said on a sob, 'I mean no, not in the way you mean.'

'Come inside,' the girl said. 'There is somewhere quiet where we can talk. We are just closing now. My name is Maria.'

'Anita,' she replied tearfully as she followed Maria inside.

They went straight up to one of the rooms which had been converted into a boudoir where their bar boys could 'entertain' their guests. Anita glanced dubiously around at the elaborate decor, but did not comment on it. Within a few minutes, Maria had coaxed the stark, unpalatable facts out of her.

'I know I've been a fool,' she concluded miserably, 'but I don't think he had to be quite so cruel.'

'No,' Maria said, her beautiful features set

142

grimly. 'Wait here a moment, Anita, while I get you a drink. There's someone I'd like you to meet.'

When she returned, it was with an almost frighteningly self-possessed young woman with cropped black hair and startlingly violet eyes.

'My name is Karen,' the woman said and, despite her somewhat awe-inspiring appearance, her voice was kind.

The suggestion of kindness was too much for Anita, and she began to cry.

'Men – it is the way they are,' Maria said, as she comforted the weeping girl. 'They like the chase, the conquest. They cannot help this.'

Karen looked at the other women steadily.

'Then we must help them, Maria. We must show them how a woman likes to be treated and train them to serve.'

'*Train* them? How?'

Both Maria and Anita stared at her, wide-eyed. Anita forgot to cry. Karen sensed the atmosphere in the room change, become charged with excitement. She felt a surge of adrenalin as she realised she'd found her first recruits.

'I'll teach you,' she promised. 'Trust me.'

Chapter Seven

*T*he first night having been such a phenomenal success, Karen knew she must now start recruiting in earnest. With Anita on a temporary work permit to help behind the bar and Dale and Peter rushed off their feet, she knew that she needed to find reinforcements – fast.

The day after the opening, she was sitting in the main square of Leventos sipping sangria and reflecting on their success when a young man took the table opposite her. He smiled at her when he caught her eye, and offered her a drink.

Karen sized him up, automatically assessing his potential. Conjuring up her most winning smile, she pinned it on to her face and said, 'Why not? I'd appreciate the company.'

She crossed her legs to reveal a lean expanse of bare, tanned thigh as the young man picked up his drink and joined her at her table.

'Another jug of Sangria?' he asked, his eyes caressing her exposed skin.

'That would be lovely,' Karen answered, openly making an inventory of her own.

He was tall, six feet at least, but slender, and probably no more than 23 or 24. His hair was bleached blond by the sun and he looked as though he was permanently squinting in the light as there were faint white creases in the skin around his eyes which the sun hadn't kissed.

'I'm Adrian,' he said, holding out his hand for her to shake as he introduced himself.

His grip was languid, his wrist limp, and he looked startled when Karen gave his hand an experimental squeeze. She smiled into his eyes, which widened as he recognised something unexpected in her gaze.

'I'm Karen,' she said, still holding his hand. Her thumb brushed sensually across the back of it, smoothing the silky blond hairs so that they were all lying in the same direction. His hands were broad, the fingers square-tipped with neat, smooth nails. Turning over the hand she was holding, Karen ran the fingertips of her free hand across the palm, noticing that it made the young man shiver.

'What do you do for a living, Adrian?' she asked him, conversationally.

'I'm a graphic artist by day, and a fine artist by night, when I get the chance!' He attempted a grin, but it seemed to come out crookedly, without carrying much conviction.

'Here on holiday?'

'Just passing through. I'm taking a year out, picking up odd jobs here and there. You?'

The waitress arrived with another jug of sangria, and Karen waited for her to leave them again before answering.

'I'm, working here, temporarily. Tell me,' she said, relinquishing his hand and pouring him a glass of sangria before refilling her own, 'do you happen to be looking for work at the moment?'

'I might be, if an opportunity presented itself.'

Karen passed him his glass and their fingers touched.

'I could do with a new barman,' she told him casually.

'Really? Are you . . . alone?' he asked her.

Karen saw the slow burn of sexual interest in his eyes and smiled to herself. This one would be easy to hook. 'I thought I was sitting here with you?'

Adrian coloured, as if she made him feel like a gauche youth. 'I didn't mean – '

'I know what you didn't mean, Adrian,' she interrupted him, leaning forward in her seat and fixing him with a level gaze. 'The question is, what *do* you mean?'

He stared at her, at a loss. Taking pity on him, Karen smiled and sat back in her seat.

'I'm a free agent, of course,' she told him, brushing the tip of her shoe up and down the inside of his shin under the table.

'Then . . . perhaps you'd like to come out for a drink sometime?'

Karen shrugged. Reaching into her purse, she drew out a business card and gave it to him.

'If you're interested in that bar work, be at this address at five o'clock sharp. I have to go now – don't be late!'

She rose, and walked briskly away from the table. Although she was aware of his eyes burning into her back as he watched her go, she did not look around, knowing she had already piqued his interest and not wanting to overdo things.

Karen knew his sort. By the time he arrived at Angels later that afternoon, he would have convinced himself that he had made all the running, and that she had been all over him. She had liked the way he looked, and the way his skin had felt under her fingers, and she knew she would enjoy discovering his own particular peccadillos. Now all she had to do was persuade Anita and Maria to take part.

'You want us to do *what*?' Maria was agog when Karen casually announced that they had their first 'trainee' arriving at five.

'You don't have to touch him if you don't want to, not the first time, but I will need you to assist me,' she explained calmly.

'I've never done anything like that before,' Anita said uncertainly.

'What makes you think *I* have?' Maria snapped. 'Honestly Karen, surely you don't expect us to pander to a complete stranger?'

'It'll be fun. Really. Come on, girls – didn't you say that you'd trust me?'

'Yes, but – '

'Then at least give it a try! It's not as if we're

147

going to let him touch any of us. You can imagine it's Ricardo, Anita – you wouldn't have any trouble wielding a crop or a whip then, would you?'

Two heated spots of colour showed high on Anita's cheeks, and her eyes were feverish as she shook her head.

'Perhaps you should bring Ricardo in for my first time, maybe that's what I need, an incentive!'

'He can wait,' Karen said shortly. 'Right now, both of you need to learn the rudiments of domination. And without being unduly conceited, you have a master – or, should I say, a mistress? – of the art to teach you. Well?'

Maria and Anita looked at each other in silence for a moment, then they turned in unison to look at Karen.

'All right,' Maria said, her jaw setting as if she was agreeing to undertake something particularly unpleasant, 'I'll do it.'

Karen smiled and looked at Anita. After a moment, the other girl nodded. 'Count me in,' she said, as if she had just made a momentous decision.

Stepping forward, Karen put her arms around both women and gave them a hug.

'It'll be fun – I promise,' she told them.

Both cast her a dubious glance.

'It had better be!' Maria said fiercely, making them all laugh.

Karen watched from the shadows as the young man she'd met earlier swaggered into the bar.

'You're late,' she said, stepping into the light.

He turned towards her, confident of his ability to

charm her. Then he saw what she was holding in her hands and his arrogance dissolved as the smile slid from his face.

'What – '

'I warned you to be on time, Adrian. Come – I have something for you.'

Adrian eyed the leather cuffs she was toying with with a mixture of curiosity and distrust as he moved towards her.

'Don't worry,' Karen reassured him as he reached her, 'I won't bite!'

Stepping forward, she kissed him, hard, on the lips. When she moved back, she saw that his eyes had darkened and he was looking at her hungrily.

'Do you like the outfit?' she asked lightly, turning on her heel to give him an all-round view.

'It's . . . very nice,' he replied dutifully.

Karen laughed. 'Very nice' was not the usual description her boys applied to the tight leather basque worn with the red velvet mini skirt and black fishnet stockings. She saw his gaze fall to the wicked spike heels of her red leather mules and suppressed a smile. He was so easy to read!

'Come,' she said, taking him by the hand, 'I know exactly what you need.'

As he walked a pace behind her, Karen sensed his unease and knew it to be caused partly by fear, partly by excitement. He was taking a step into the unknown and, whilst fully conscious of that fact, he still harboured the belief that he would remain in control, both of himself and of the situation.

Karen knew that this belief was no more than a fragile illusion. She also knew that learning the truth would, ultimately, give him a kind of freedom he had never experienced before, a kind of freedom that he had never dreamt existed. As they walked, she was mentally formulating a plan, a personalised timetable for his initiation.

Anita and Maria were waiting for them in the black room. Adrian's eyes widened as he looked around, taking in the decor and then fixing his gaze on the metal couch which had been placed to one side of the centre of the room. On the other side, two large plaster pillars, topped at shoulder height by carved horses' heads, stood sentinel, about six feet apart. Through its nose, each horse had a large metal ring which glittered in the dim electric light.

'Wh-what's going on?' he stuttered.

'Your interview, darling,' Karen said, running her forefinger down his smooth cheek. 'I'd like to introduce you to Maria and Anita – don't you think they look pretty?'

She had dressed Anita in shiny white PVC from head to toe – a sleeveless A-line mini dress, white stockings and knee-high white boots with neat, square heels. Anita had then skilfully accentuated the look with heavy black kohl around her eyes and false eyelashes, and her lips were painted the palest of pale pinks, shimmering in the light.

Maria was resplendent in a black silk camisole and French knickers. Her shiny black stockings were held up with tiny suspenders which emerged from beneath the bottom edges of the French knickers, and her small feet were encased in feathered mules with impossibly high heels.

150

Adrian looked from one to the other of them, as if unable to believe his own eyes.

'This is a joke, right?' He laughed nervously.

'No joke,' Karen purred.

As he stared around him, Karen wrapped one of the silk-lined leather cuffs around his wrist, pulling the straps tight and fastening the buckles. Adrian jumped as if he had been scalded.

'What are you doing?' he asked, foolishly.

Karen disregarded his question, and merely moved around to his other arm and fastened the second cuff to his wrist.

'Look, I'm not so sure – '

'Ssh!' Karen said, placing her fingers against his lips. 'You're free to leave at any time,' she explained, softly. 'You only have to say the word, and we will let you go. But I don't think you want to go yet, do you, Adrian? I think you're too curious, too excited to leave right now. You want to know what we're going to do with you, don't you? More than you've ever wanted anything, *ever*. And if you leave here, you'll never know how pleasurable it could have been . . .'

It was as if her words had hypnotised him, for Adrian stood rigidly in the centre of the room, his eyes darting between the three women as if he was desperate to keep all of them in his line of vision at all times. Karen could feel the tension in the way he held himself, and she knew that he would not be able to tear himself away, not now. Probably not ever.

'Isn't this one of your most secret fantasies, Adrian? That three women want to pleasure you all at the same time? We know just how to divine your deepest, darkest desires, even the most shameful of them. Oh yes, *particularly* the most shameful of them! Isn't that right, ladies?'

'That's right,' Maria mumbled unconvincingly, her eyes fixed on the floor.

Surprisingly, it was Anita who bit the bullet, shy, quiet Anita who threw herself into the role in which she had initially been so reluctant to be cast.

'That's right, Karen,' she said, moving forward so that she could strut around the man now standing alone in the middle of the room. 'You were right – he *is* pretty,' she said. 'But can he control himself? Does he have any self-discipline? I doubt it.'

'He will have when he leaves here,' Karen said. 'Take off your clothes, Adrian, let's take a look at you.'

He caught her eye and stared at her. For a moment, Karen thought he might actually lose his nerve and walk out, but then she saw, at the back of his eyes the same light which she had spotted when he had approached her earlier that day, and her confidence that he would stay increased.

Holding her gaze, he curled his fingers under the hem of his T-shirt and peeled it off over his head. The tension in the room heightened as he revealed a youthful torso, thin, but manly, with a line of red-blond hair travelling from his sternum down to his navel. Little wisps circled the flat, brown discs of his nipples, which hardened on contact with the air.

Anita stepped forward and took the T-shirt from

him without a word. Karen glanced towards his jeans, and his fingers hovered over the fly-fastening.

'What are you going to do?' he asked her, his voice hoarse with suppressed excitement.

'You'll see. The jeans?'

Adrian unfastened his jeans, slipping each button through its stiff buttonhole whilst his eyes moved slowly from Karen to Anita to Maria and back again, his expression a mixture of fear and desire. His legs were strong, his thighs long and slender. Under his jeans, he was wearing a pair of plain white Calvin Klein boxer shorts.

'Those too,' Karen said when he hesitated.

'And the socks,' Anita said, coming to life at the sight of his denim-blue socks, still on his feet. 'Why do men never take off their socks before they pull down their trousers? Don't they know how *pathetic* they look in just their socks? How much of a turn-off?'

Maria stared at Anita as if she had just heard a fieldmouse bark, but Karen merely smiled. She was glad that Anita was warming up – she sure as hell couldn't take on the number of men they required by herself.

'Didn't you hear the lady?' she snapped, as Adrian, still in his socks, stood and stared incredulously at Anita, his hands cupping his semi-erection. 'Get them off!'

He jumped to do her bidding, his prick bobbing frantically at right angles to his body as he bent over. The three women glanced at each other, and Karen gave the others an encouraging wink. They hadn't been at all keen at first, but she sensed that now they had a real, live man in front of them, their interest had quickened.

At last, Adrian stood before them, naked and exposed, his vulnerability plain for all to see. He looked miserable, as if he really didn't know what the hell to do, and Karen allowed her lip to curl into a sneer.

'Look at you!' she said, walking around him. 'Three women at your disposal, and you don't know where to start! The truth is, you haven't got the balls for it, have you?'

'Karen – '

'Shut up!'

His eyes widened in shock, but he remained silent.

'Strap him up,' she said, turning her back as Anita and Maria moved forward.

When Karen turned back again, Adrian's arms had been fastened, by the chains dangling from each leather cuff, to each of the rings through the horses' noses. Together, the two other women operated the pulley which moved the statuary along the floor to the point at which his arms were stretched out at shoulder level.

Adrian's eyes held real fear now, and Karen smiled. This was better – a little healthy fear never went amiss in a situation like this. Standing squarely before him, she ran her palms across her upper body, cupping her leather-encased breasts and licking her lips lasciviously. Adrian's eyes were like saucers and he leant forward slightly, only to be frustrated by his restraints.

'You'd like to, wouldn't you, Adrian?' Karen said softly. 'You'd like to touch me like this . . .'

She eased one breast out of her basque and squeezed the areola between her finger and thumb. The rosy nipple sprang to life and Adrian groaned softly. Looking down, Karen saw that his erection had grown, and she covered her breast away again, business-like now, moved back and regarded him thoughtfully.

He had a nice cock, straight and long with a smooth, circumcised tip which, as she watched, oozed a teardrop of fluid.

'Now this will never do,' Karen said, pulling out a tissue from the box she kept to hand, and wiping the droplet away.

At the touch of the tissue against his cock-tip, Adrian let out a long, shuddering sigh. At a pre-arranged signal, Maria stepped forward with a soft suede pouch.

'The object of today, Adrian, is to teach you to control your responses. There'll be time enough for the rest, later. Now, as it's your first time, you may be told in advance some of the lessons you are to be taught. The first is that pleasure delayed is pleasure doubled. Do you understand that, Adrian?'

'Yes,' he replied, blinking rapidly as he waited for her to go on.

'I doubt that very much,' Karen replied contemptuously, 'but you will learn. Maria?'

Maria stepped forward and, taking his tumescent shaft between her finger and thumb, a fastidious expression on her face, she eased the suede pouch over it.

'Jesus!' he cried, as she bent his erection downward in order to strap the pouch to his leg.

Karen stepped forward. 'Steady,' she whispered to Maria, 'don't yank it, *ease* it down.'

She signalled to Anita and watched as the blonde girl brought the silk-lined black leather mask over to her. Karen picked it up and showed it to Adrian.

'I find that if one of the senses is denied, the others all clamour to compensate,' she said.

'I don't think – '

Karen picked up the crop she had ready and flicked it across his belly. The small, stinging pain shocked him into silence.

'I don't want to know what you think. If you speak again before being spoken to, I'll have you gagged as well. Understand?'

He nodded vigorously, making her smile.

'You learn fast. That's good,' she told him, running her fingers lightly over the skin that the crop had kissed. 'I like a man who knows when to do as he's told.'

Anita had to stand on a small stool to fasten the eye mask around Adrian's head. When she had done this, Karen stepped forward and, keeping her body so close to his that she knew he could feel the heat of her, she ran her fingertips gently around the edges of the mask.

Close to, she could see the nervous perspiration seeping through his pores. His lips parted and trembled, lending his masked face a certain vulnerable beauty which moved her. Slowly, she touched her lips lightly against his, moving them tenderly back and forth so that little shivers of pleasure ran through his veins. His teeth parted and Karen probed his mouth with her tongue, seeking out the most sensitive spots to stimulate whilst pressing her body even harder against his.

She imagined how the soft leather encasing her torso would feel against his naked skin, and she shivered. Against her velvet-clad upper thigh, she could feel the urgent pressure of his restrained cock between his tense legs.

'Endure, my love,' she whispered softly, as she broke the kiss. 'Let go of yourself. You'll soon discover how sweet it is . . .'

He sighed, a long, juddering sigh that spoke volumes. Karen stepped back and glanced at the other woman. Anita was gazing at her in awe, her eyes wide. Maria's eyes, on the other hand, had darkened and Karen saw the spark of arousal in their depths. She raised a quizzical brow in Maria's direction, but Maria looked away, keeping her thoughts to herself.

'Well, ladies,' Karen said briskly. 'Time to begin!'

Maria watched through her eyelashes as Karen wheeled out the trolley she had prepared earlier. The Spanish girl's stomach was churning with arousal and her legs felt too weak to support her as she ran her eyes over the contents, which had been laid out neatly, as though they were surgical instruments.

There was a long, slim vibrator beside a large pot of lubricating cream, the crop Karen had used earlier, a long-handled whip, the end of which was split into some half dozen wispy-looking tails, and a squat leather item which looked rather like a table tennis bat. Maria's eyes, though, came to rest on the thin, whippy cane beside it, and the sight of it alone was enough to start a pulse beating between her legs.

It had been six weeks since her last visit to Julio Escobar, and since then they had communicated only by telephone. Last time they had spoken, the old man had confirmed her suspicion that he did not wish her to visit again and, although she had since sent him a freshly worn pair of panties, she respected his decision. He was clearly too old and too ill to continue to concern himself with her 'salvation'. But what was she going to do now that Escobar was not on hand to bring her darkest fantasies into the light?

She had seen the way Karen had looked at her. Had she guessed? Maria's cheeks burned with shame as she contemplated the idea of her friend knowing the truth.

'Maria?'

Her head snapped up at Karen's soft call and her gaze clashed with her all-knowing violet eyes. She saw the reflection of her own desire in Karen's pupils and sucked in her breath. Oh God, surely this desire which seared her could not be directed at Karen?

Anita laid a hand softly on her shoulder and Maria jumped as if it had burned her. Turning to the other girl, she saw that she, too, was looking at her with empathy, and she realised that it was not

158

so much Karen she desired – she was merely the channel by which Maria could realise her fantasies – but Anita, with her soft, plump flesh, and her undemanding, fluffy ways.

Maria's lips trembled as she moved towards Anita and kissed her, lightly, on the mouth. It was the first time Maria had ever kissed another woman and she savoured the moment, recognising in Anita an echo of her own desire. She guessed it was also a first for the other girl, for, as they moved apart, Anita's soft, sherry-brown eyes reflected her surprise.

There was, however, no disgust, nor any horror, nor any other of the negative reactions that Maria might have expected, and a spark of hope was struck in her heart. She had never felt this way towards a man before – maybe she had simply been looking for love in the wrong place.

Both of them turned as Karen cleared her throat. She was regarding them both with a look of mild amusement, but, Maria noticed, with no sign of surprise. Had she been able to divine their inclination before either she or Anita had realised it themselves?

Slowly, she became aware once more of the naked man, bound and blindfolded, waiting patiently in the middle of the room, temporarily forgotten.

'We could simply walk out and leave him here, but it would be rather a waste, don't you think?' Karen whispered.

Maria smiled.

'A terrible waste,' she agreed, pulling herself together.

Smiling at her, Karen handed her a bottle of oil.

'Make him slippery,' she said, rolling her tongue around the word in a way that was designed to lighten the tension which had gripped them all.

Anita, too, took a bottle of oil and the two women smeared it over Adrian's skin, taking a side each. Catching Anita's eye, Maria felt as though they were caressing each other through the man, and she felt her sex becoming heavy and moist. Now that she had noticed Anita in this way, she knew she would have to explore this new facet to her sexual personality, and she hoped fervently that the blonde girl would be willing.

Anita looked so sweet in her 60s-style white PVC get-up. Maria imagined herself peeling it away from her plump, fragrant flesh, and her fingers moved more sensually across Adrian's thighs, causing him to moan softly.

'Is that good, darling?' Karen asked him silkily, running her long fingers over his chest.

'Ahh,' he replied, capable of no more than a long, drawn-out sigh.

'You see?' Karen crooned. 'It isn't so bad, is it? Not as bad as you feared?'

Maria watched as she picked up the short-handled leather paddle and strolled around behind him. Adrian relaxed, the tension leaving his limbs as he listened to her soft, soothing voice and revelled in the touch of the other two women as they worked the oil into his skin.

Karen waited until they had finished before signalling to them to move aside. Then she brought the paddle down with a slap against Adrian's buttocks, making him cry out in shock.

'Jesus! What was that?'

Karen tutted theatrically, putting her lips close to his ear so that he could feel her warm breath brushing his cheek as she spoke.

'What did I say we'd have to do if you spoke without permission?'

'But –'

'*What did I say*?'

'You said you would gag me,' he whispered.

Karen kissed him lightly down the side of his face, darting her tongue into the whorls of his ear and making him shiver.

'Is that what you were wanting, Adrian? To be gagged? Is that one of your fantasies?'

'No! Please – I don't want it . . .'

Karen reached round to feel the tumescence of his cock in its soft suede restraint.

'I think you protest too much,' she said, squeezing gently at his painfully constricted shaft. 'The cock never lies!'

Maria and Anita moved closer together, their fingers entwining as they stood side by side. Maria found watching Karen at work fascinating, seeing an echo of Escobar's initial manipulation of her in Karen's methods.

When he had first arrived, she had thought that this young man would have refused to consent to any of the games Karen had in store for him. Karen must have seen something in him, some part of his character that predisposed him to taking pleasure through pain and humiliation – just as Escobar had seen something in her.

At a sign from Karen, Maria left Anita and went to fetch the gag which had been laid out ready on the trolley. It was made of supple black leather, with two metal rings either side of a malleable black ball. She imagined the taste of the leather pressing down her tongue and shivered involuntarily. Escobar had never thought to gag her, but then, for him, restricted as he was by age and, of course, his blindness and infirmity, hearing her cry and beg had been a great part of the pleasure he had derived from the games they had played.

Karen ran her fingertips along Adrian's lips, so that he opened them voluntarily. Then she kissed him, and Maria could see her tongue insinuating itself between his teeth, making his jaw slacken and his mouth open wider.

Moving her head away, she took the ball-gag from Maria, and eased it between his lips. Adrian made a strangled noise of protest, but Karen ignored him, fastening the buckle tightly at the back of his head and running her finger around the perimeter of the device to check that it wasn't too tight for him to breathe.

'There,' she said, with a wink at Maria, 'that's better! Let it go, darling, just let it go . . .'

Her hands soothed him before she moved in behind him again and smacked him several more times with the paddle. Maria went to stand next to her, and watched his white skin redden with fascination.

'Would you like to try?' Karen asked, offering her the paddle.

Maria's eyes slid to the cane which was on the trolley.

'I'd rather use this,' she said, her fingers closing round it.

Karen's eyebrows rose, but she did not comment as she nodded and stepped aside.

Maria swiped the air experimentally, making Adrian flinch. She knew exactly how he felt, and she repeated the manoeuvre purely to heighten the sense of anticipation. It felt odd to her to find herself preparing to administer the punishment to come, rather than waiting to receive it.

Her hand shook as she positioned herself behind Adrian and raised the cane. His buttocks were glowing after the spanking they had received from the paddle, and Maria felt her own flesh throb in sympathy. She knew how the shock of pain would by now have subsided, lessening to a dull ache and then, ultimately, to a warm, spreading pleasure.

Everyone was waiting for her – Adrian tautly, anticipating further pain before the onset of bliss, and Karen and Anita expectantly, both eager to see how she would deal with him. For her part, Maria was wishing more than anything that the roles were reversed: that it was she who was tethered to the rings, blindfolded, gagged and waiting for the bittersweet, biting kiss of the cane across her buttocks. The cane suddenly felt heavy in her hand and she dropped it on the ground with a clatter.

'I can't!' she gasped, her voice breaking on a sob.

'It's all right,' Karen said, and her voice was filled

with kindness. Walking over to Maria, she put her arm around her shoulders and drew her away.

It was then that Maria realised that Anita had retrieved the cane from where it had fallen, and that she was standing in position, waiting for a signal from Karen before she began . . .

Chapter Eight

*T*here was a new light in Anita's eyes that made her look different, self-assured in a way that made Maria's pulse race. Her face had hardened and taken on a forbidding cast and her light brown eyes had darkened to the colour of chocolate as she looked to Karen for permission to continue.

'Go on,' Karen said softly, with an almost maternal pride, 'you take over now, Anita.'

Adrian pulled against his bonds and made a strangled sound at the back of his throat. Walking over to Maria, Anita placed the cane gently in her hands. Maria's fingers gripped it tightly, her knuckles showing white through her olive skin. Anita went back to the trolley and, after a few moments' thought, selected a long, black feather from it.

At the shock of the first touch of the feather against his cringing skin, Adrian sucked in his breath. He made another muffled noise behind the ball-gag, and Karen stepped forward to unfasten it, judging that the sound of his gasps and sighs would add to the women's pleasure. Glancing from Anita to Maria, she saw they were both highly aroused, and she quietly moved to the metal couch, which, unnoticed by them, she covered in a generous layer of soft, peacock-blue velvet.

Anita ran the feather across Adrian's chest, twirling it around his nipples, which hardened into two aching little peaks, straining towards her. Dipping the end of the feather into the indentation of his navel, Anita then swept it down over his oiled belly. His cock twitched in its soft suede pouch, and Anita glanced towards Karen.

'Can I take this off?' she asked.

Karen raised her eyebrows. 'If you like, but he'll come very quickly if he isn't restrained,' she warned.

'That's all right. Maria, come and release his cock.'

Maria jumped at the note of command in Anita's voice and, putting the cane down on the floor, she rushed to do her bidding.

Adrian gave a juddering sigh of relief as his penis sprang free. Immediately, it engorged with blood, his erection rising proudly from his groin, the circumcised bulb gleaming an angry purplish-red.

'Now go and fetch me the cane,' Anita said.

Maria's hands trembled as she obeyed. As she handed the cane to Anita, she caught the other girl's eye. Her breath seemed to catch in her chest as she recognised the dominant glitter in the blonde girl's eyes, and she felt a sudden mule's kick of undiluted desire deep in the pit of her stomach.

Anita slapped the cane lightly against her own bare thigh, and Maria's eyes widened as the skin pinkened along the line of her blow.

'Take his blindfold off,' she said curtly.

Maria once again rushed to obey, excitement rushing through her veins.

Adrian blinked as his eyes grew used to the light, and he searched for Karen. His expression was anguished, though undeniably aroused, and she relished the sight of the battle he was clearly fighting with himself. She knew he couldn't hope to win it, though he would continue to fight to hold himself in check until the bitter end. There were very few men who could accept that total submission to a woman was the key to their true sexual fulfilment. She smiled at him, injecting into her expression a shade of sympathy, which he grasped eagerly.

'Kneel,' Anita said, tapping Maria's buttocks with the end of her cane.

Maria sank to her knees with alacrity, waiting meekly for Anita's further instructions.

'I want you to suck him,' she said. 'Suck him until he comes.'

Maria's eyes widened in shock, but nevertheless she shuffled forward on her knees so that she was kneeling at Adrian's feet, her eyes level with his cock.

She had never fellated a man before. His penis looked huge and ugly. There were thick veins standing out on the shaft, the glans was smooth and shiny, glowing an angry red, and the small eye in its centre wept a teardrop of fluid.

'Lick it clean,' Anita barked.

Maria put out her tongue experimentally and dabbed at the tear of clear fluid. It tasted salty, slightly milky, and warm. Reaching for his cock, she prepared to take the bulb into her mouth, but Anita flicked the cane once more across her buttocks.

'No hands,' she snapped. Put your hands behind your back where I can see them.'

Maria clasped her hands behind her, aware with her every nerve-ending, with every fibre of her being, that Anita was watching her, running her eyes over her body in a way no woman had ever done before.

'Now,' Anita said, leaning forward to press her lips against Maria's hair, 'take him in your mouth, and suck him dry.'

He was big: stretching her lips wide, Maria felt her jaw protest as she drew him into the heated confines of her mouth. She sensed that he was holding his breath, that the feel of her soft lips enclosing him was driving him crazy with desire.

Anita walked around behind him again and raised the cane. It came down with a loud crack across his buttocks and Maria felt him jerk, deep into her throat, making her gag and pull back with a choked cry of protest.

Anita grabbed him by the hair and pulled his head back so that he could look into her eyes.

'Don't you ever do that again,' she hissed through gritted teeth. 'That girl deserves respect, and if she doesn't get it then it will be the worse for you. Understand?'

'Yes,' he gasped, tears springing to his eyes as she released him.

'Maybe we should start a chart like the one they keep at the Bar del Amore,' Anita said to Karen. 'This one wouldn't score very highly.'

Karen hid a smile. Who would have thought that Anita, quiet, mousy Anita who, only a day or so before, wouldn't have said 'boo' to anyone, would possess such a talent for domination and humiliation? Glancing at Maria, she saw that the other girl was gazing at Anita with a look of complete adoration on her lovely face. Karen shook her head in wonder. When Ricardo found out about this . . .

'Take him back into your mouth, Maria – and this time, suck him dry.'

Maria sucked greedily on Adrian's distended shaft. Her breasts thrust forward against the silk of her camisole and her sex lips swelled and rubbed against her French knickers. She could feel the excitement of the man bound in front of her, and sensed that he was holding back, desperately trying not to thrust savagely into her mouth as he had done before.

Anita applied the cane across his buttocks several times, each time being careful not to touch the stripe she had made before. When she judged that he was close to coming, she brought the cane down hard across his thighs, making sure that it hurt him this time, so that he would begin to associate the receiving of pain with eruption of pleasure.

He cried out as his ejaculate gushed along his

shaft and into Maria's waiting mouth. She lapped at the hot, salty liquid, trying desperately to swallow it all, even as she was aware of it running from the corners of her mouth, streaking her chin, and dripping on to the upward curve of her breasts.

Ignoring Adrian, who was still thrusting his hips back and forth even after Maria had pulled away, Anita went over to the girl and caressed her cheeks.

'You spilt some, darling,' she said softly, bowing her head to lick the stray drops from the corners of Maria's mouth. 'I shall have to punish you for that.'

'Yes,' Maria said, trembling, 'please . . .'

Karen bent to kiss each of them on the cheek. 'I'll just move him out of the way,' she whispered, tipping her head towards Adrian.

The two women watched as she released him from his bonds and led him from the room.

'What's she going to do?' Maria whispered.

Anita caressed the top of her head. 'I should imagine she will take him through the next stage of his training,' she replied. 'Now that he has learnt to obey, he can be taught how to give the most pleasure, and how to subjugate his own desires in order to satisfy the woman he's with. Of course,' she continued, with a smile, 'he will also learn, in time, that his own pleasure will be heightened tenfold when he has learnt to make a woman truly willing.'

Maria looked up at her, a look of wonder on her face.

'How is it that you know so much about this? Did Karen tell you what she had planned beforehand?'

Anita looked thoughtful, her hand still stroking the crown of Maria's head as the other girl knelt at her feet.

'I think it's an instinct,' she said slowly, 'because somehow I knew exactly what it was that man wanted – just as I know exactly what it is you want, Maria, my love.' She looked straight at Maria, making her tremble afresh.

'What – what I want?' Maria echoed, sounding a little confused.

Anita smiled slowly, sending shivers of delicious apprehension up and down the other girl's spine.

'Yes. Down on all fours – bum high, please.'

Maria obeyed at once, leaning heavily on her forearms and pushing her hips up and back, so that the silk of her French knickers was stretched tautly across her buttocks. Anita drew them down over her parted thighs until they were pulled tight between her knees, exposing the smooth, caramel flesh of her bottom.

'So beautiful,' she murmured, her hand caressing the firm, globes of Maria's buttocks. 'So smooth and tight, yet succulent, like a ripe peach ...'

Maria gasped as Anita reached unexpectedly between her legs, running her fingers lightly along the cleft of her arse, over the hot well of moisture and up to tweak her clitoris.

'Mmm – wet, too. What a bad, bad girl you are, Maria! Did it turn you on, sucking that cock?'

'No,' Maria whispered.

'No? Then how do you account for this?'

Anita delved into the hot, wet sheath of Maria's

171

sex and then held her moisture-slicked fingers under the girl's nose.

'Suck,' she said, softly.

Maria sucked each of her fingers in turn, cleansing them of her juices, and tasting the musky tang of her own body for the first time.

'That's good, isn't it?' Anita whispered, her hot lips close to Maria's ear. 'Are you still telling me you didn't enjoy sucking that cock?'

'I enjoyed it knowing you were watching me,' Maria admitted at last.

Anita smiled. 'Good girl,' she said, poking her tongue into Maria's ear and following the contours within it. 'I'll reward you later, if you take your punishment well.'

She rose then and, taking up the cane, she stood behind Maria. Maria tensed, waiting for the kiss of the implement across her bottom. Even so, she wasn't prepared for the sudden pain as Anita brought it down with relish.

'Oh!' she cried aloud, 'Oh, Anita, that hurt!'

Anita rubbed her stinging flesh with a soft hand, but then she brought the cane down again, slightly lower this time, so that Maria felt her flesh shiver and shake under the impact.

'Oh, please – that's a little bit too hard!'

'Really?' Anita sounded bored. 'Then I guess you'll have to do your penance by giving me some pleasure instead, then, Maria. Maybe you could use your mouth – you used it effectively enough on Adrian.'

Maria looked up in alarm. It had never before occurred to her that the prospect of performing

172

cunnilingus could give her any pleasure, but she could not deny that a fresh rush of moisture was staining her inner thighs even as Anita spoke.

Still on all fours, she watched as the blonde girl went over to the velvet-covered couch and, putting the cane aside, leant against it. Holding Maria's eye, she hitched her short white PVC skirt up above her waist and slid her boot-shod feet apart. Maria could see the pale blonde thatch of hair covering her mons and, below it, the delicate pink slit of her sex, its folds of flesh opening and glistening as Anita parted her thighs.

'Crawl over here,' she said, her pupils dilating as she watched Maria obey. 'God, I wish you could see yourself, Maria – you look fantastic! Now, bury your face in between my legs and start licking.'

Maria breathed in the perfume of Anita's sex, and felt her own labia becoming puffy and moist in direct response to the olfactory stimulus. Tentatively, she pushed out her tongue and licked along the glistening channel. It tasted quite pleasant: a kind of salty-sweetness coated her lips and tongue and she set about her task with enthusiasm. Working on the theory that what felt good to her would probably feel good to Anita, too, she flicked her tongue lightly across the hard little nub at the apex of her labia, before delving into the dark recess of her vagina.

'Jesus, Maria, you're good at this!' Anita breathed, bending her legs slightly to allow her deeper access.

Maria probed the hot, elastic tube that led into Anita's body, feeling the ridged walls contract around her stiffened tongue, drawing it further in. Taking a chance that she wouldn't be told not to use her hands, as she had been with Adrian, she placed them on Anita's inner thighs, stroking the fine, soft flesh and digging her fingers into the plump curve of her bottom, tilting her pelvis slightly so that she could push her tongue yet further inside.

Encouraged by Anita's increasingly enthusiastic moans, Maria grasped her by her hips and rubbed her face against her sex, butting her nose against the hard little button of her clitoris whilst thrusting her tongue in and out of her hot little hole.

With a cry, Anita tipped over into orgasm. Her legs scissored around Maria's head and shoulders and her clitoris spasmed wildly, pulsing with the strength of her climax. Pressing the flat of her tongue against it, Maria felt the rush of honeyed secretions wash over her lips, and she moaned deeply.

Anita reached down and drew her lover up so that she could kiss her. Her tongue swept around Maria's lips and chin, then thrust into her open mouth as she put her arms around her and helped her up on to the couch. Maria gasped as she felt Anita's hand dispense with her knickers and begin to stroke her inner thigh.

'It's all right, baby,' Anita whispered. 'Trust me. I know what you want ... I know what you need ...'

Her fingers unerringly found the aching nub of her clitoris and she rubbed gently, moving it around beneath the skin until Maria, too, peaked, crying out and hugging Anita to her as her body was wracked by spasm after spasm of bliss.

'I never knew . . .' she cried, when she had regained her breath. 'I never dreamt . . .!'

Anita laughed. 'Me neither! I've never thought to even look at another woman in that way before.'

They stared at each other solemnly.

'Do you think it will last?' Maria asked.

'We can try. At least we know the things we shouldn't say or do to each other!'

Maria smiled. Anita was far more experienced with men than she was, yet now she felt certain that she had found what she had been looking for. 'That's true,' she said, reaching out to stroke Anita's face. 'And we also know exactly what feels good, at least in theory.'

'Absolutely!' Anita agreed, laughing. 'And we're sure as hell going to have a lot of fun putting theory into practice!'

Darren brought the new bar boys straight to Ricardo at his house when he collected them from the airport. Ricardo looked at them and knew at once that the romantic-looking, black-haired Irishman was perfect for what he had in mind.

'I want you to work for a rival bar,' he told him, once he had sent his companion on to the Bar del Amore with Darren. 'Obviously, you will report back to me exactly what they are trying to do, and why all the female tourists are flocking there.'

Ronan Doherty nodded, pushing back his floppy black hair with an impatient gesture. 'There'll be more money in this for me then, I take it,' he said.

'Yes, there will be more money. Provided you keep your mouth shut and tell no one but me what you find out. Angels is run by an Englishwoman called Karen – she's the person you need to contact about her advertisement for male staff. Any questions?'

Ronan shrugged. 'Not at the moment. How do I contact you?'

'I'll give you my phone number here. I expect to hear from you in a few days.'

The two men rose and shook hands. As he watched Ronan ride away on the scooter he had provided, Ricardo told himself that he had set in motion a counter-attack against Karen and Maria which would bring them both back into line.

That idea gave him a great deal of satisfaction. He felt his cock stir as it always did lately, whenever he thought of Karen. He didn't know what she was playing at, but he still wanted her, and he was fairly sure that the feeling was mutual.

'One day,' he said aloud, staring out to the horizon across the sapphire-blue sea, 'our time will come. I will be ready for you, Karen, and this time there will be no running away – not for either of us.'

Karen eyed the new recruit to Angels with interest. Pale-skinned, green-eyed and roguishly charming, Ronan was just the kind of man she wanted to educate to treat women better. He'd answered all her questions about past relationships and his attitudes to the girls he had bedded with a candour that would have taken her breath away had he not been so depressingly typical.

'Well, Ronan,' she said, sitting back in her chair in the small back room she had turned into an office, 'you've been honest with me about yourself, now let me tell you a little about the idea behind Angels.

'We're running a bar here which caters purely for women on holiday, plus one or two locals who are quickly becoming regulars. These women want to relax, have a drink with friends and, if they feel like it, good casual sex.'

'It sounds like the Bar del Amore,' Ronan said, when she paused.

Karen's eyes narrowed suspiciously. 'What do you know about the Bar del Amore?' she asked watching him closely.

Ronan cursed his loose tongue as he summoned a grin which was designed to disarm. 'Everyone's heard of the Bar of Love in Dublin – it's one of the most desirable summer jobs in the Med.'

'I see.' Karen tightened her lips. 'Let me tell you, Ronan, Angels is nothing like the Bar del Amore. After the obvious purpose of lining Señor Baddeiras' pockets, that place is run largely for the benefit of the studs he employs in the bar.'

'But isn't that what the women who go there want? A good shag with no strings attached?' he asked.

Karen's eyes glittered dangerously at him across the table. She was going to take a personal interest in training this one!

177

'Do you like women, Ronan?' she asked, her voice dangerously soft.

He looked affronted. 'Of course I do! I'm no fag, I –'

'I mean, really like them. For example, describe your ideal woman to me.'

He shrugged. 'Tall, long legs – I like long legs – big tits –'

'Fat women, you mean?'

Ronan's face registered disgust. 'Not fat women, no.'

'But you like big breasts. Women with a high proportion of body fat usually have big breasts,' she reasoned.

'Aye, but they usually have fat arses too. I don't like squashy bums.'

'So, you like, what – Pamela Anderson lookalikes?'

Ronan grinned, feeling that he was on safer ground. 'She'll do on a dark night,' he quipped.

Karen nodded. 'Do you enjoy eating pussy, Ronan?' she said, leaning seductively towards him.

He looked decidedly alarmed. 'Well ... yeah, if she's clean and –'

'If she's sanitised, forced into fantasy woman mode. You don't *like* women, Ronan, you don't really like us at all. Our bodies repel you even while you crave access to them. You're only comfortable with a woman who conforms to your distorted idea of what is "beautiful". Don't look so worried, Ronan, after all, you're pretty typical of many men. But, if you want this job, you're going

178

to have to learn to *love* women – everything about us.'

Leaning across the table, she kissed him, delicately, on the lips, softening her harsh words with a sensuality which enthralled him, and lulled him into a false sense of security.

'Still interested?' she murmured, allowing him a good look down the front of her blouse.

He looked up into her eyes and she saw a spark of masculine defiance which excited her.

'I'm still interested,' he said.

He thought he could have her, she realised, hiding a smile. He thought that if he went along with what she said, he'd get into her knickers in double-quick time and then be off down the pub recounting the tale to his mates even faster. Lord, taming this one was going to be satisfying.

'Then let me tell you more about Angels. The women who come here, to my bar, are guaranteed discretion and unlimited satisfaction. Our training ensures that. The question is, Ronan, are you prepared to put yourself through that training?'

She watched as his eyes passed speculatively over her, signalling his belief that she would be his whenever he decided to honour her with his attention. He had a surprise in store.

'It sounds like an experience,' he said, with a twinkle in his green eyes, 'and I like to try out new experiences.'

'Very well.' Karen was brisk. She had interviewed a dozen new men in the past week and she was eager now to take some time out and to go and get some fresh air. 'Sign the contract where I've marked it for you.'

Like the others, he didn't bother to read what he was signing. Would he have been so eager had he realised he was relinquishing his right to sue if the training got too much for him? Did he realise he was agreeing to live at the club for the duration of his contract, that he was waiving virtually all his basic rights to privacy and his choice of sexual partners?

Karen doubted it. If this had been a more permanent venture, she would have taken pains to explain the terms of his contract to him. As it was, she knew that four weeks was bearable, and that, ultimately, he was not likely to complain. Most men relished paying obeisance to her by the end of a week under her tutelage.

All he wanted to know was how long he was to be bound by the contract.

'Four weeks,' she told him, eager to get away.

'Is it renewable after that?'

'No.'

'Can I ask why? I had intended to stay in Tierra del Sol for the rest of the season.'

'You'll just have to make sure that I'll be giving you a good reference, then. I can assure you that, after training here, you'll be snapped up by another employer.'

'But why four weeks?' he persisted, even after she rose, indicating that the interview was over.

'Because that's how long we intend to stay open,' she told him curtly. 'In four weeks time, Angels will cease to exist and the developers will move in to turn this place into a hotel. Come back at five – and be prepared to stay here afterwards.'

She walked out, leaving him clutching his copy of his contract, a look of consternation on his face.

Ricardo read through the contract swiftly, his quick mind immediately homing in on the unusual terms.

'My God, you've signed your life away here,' he told Ronan.

'What do you mean?' The boy frowned, taking a deep draught of his beer before giving Ricardo his full attention.

'This says you must live at the Angels bar, that you cannot leave without, I quote, "express permission from your mistresses". Do you know what that means?'

Ronan shrugged. 'There'll be ways round that. The bird who interviewed me was pretty sure of herself, though – she has a way of looking at you that's quite scary, if you know what I mean.'

Ricardo smiled grimly. 'I know exactly what you mean.'

'I bet she's great in the sack, though, eh? Have you had her?'

Ricardo felt his face tighten up. 'Do not overstep the mark, my friend,' he said quietly. 'Is this it? Do you have any other information for me?'

'Oh, yeah – I almost forgot. You noticed that contract was only for four weeks?'

Ricardo shrugged. 'That is standard practice – a renewable short-term contract gives both employer and staff a way out if they don't get on.'

'Aye, but that one's not renewable. I think you

181

might be worrying for nothing, Mr Baddeiras. Angels is only planning to stay open for another four weeks.'

Ricardo stared at him, not understanding. 'Excuse me?'

'Apparently, the place is being turned into a hotel, so there's no permanent threat to your business at all. I take it there'll be a job here for me when my contract with Angels runs out?'

'What?' Ricardo said, distracted by this latest revelation. 'Oh, yes of course. You've done well, Ronan. You can use the upstairs room to get some sleep before you have to go back at five.'

'Thanks. Be seeing you.'

Walking over to the window with Ronan's contract in his hand, Ricardo stared across at Angels, his mind racing. What did all this mean? He had assumed that Maria and Karen had set up a permanent venture, probably as some sort of revenge on him personally. Now Ronan was telling him it was for only another four weeks, which made eight weeks in total.

As he watched, the door of the bar opposite opened and Karen came through it. She was wearing a light, white cotton blouse, through which he could see the outline of a bikini top, and cut-off denim shorts. Her long legs were tanned and slender, her bare feet pushed into gleaming white pumps. Even her hair, cropped so short against her head, shone under the sun, and Ricardo found himself longing to touch it.

He swore impatiently at himself and watched as she climbed into her hire-car. She was so beautiful, like a dark, avenging angel, sent to earth to torment him. What in the world had possessed her, after all these years, to come back and confront him with an infidelity that had taken place ten years before? He loved her, wanted her, hated her, all in equal measure.

As she drove off towards the coast road, he gave in to the urge to follow her. He didn't know what she was playing at, but he was sure as hell going to find out, one way or another, once and for all.

As she drove along the coast road, Karen took a call from Aaron on her mobile phone.

'I've booked myself on a flight in a fortnight,' he told her, barely suppressed excitement colouring his tone.

'You're coming over here? Why?' she asked bluntly. The last thing she needed was a proprietorial inspection by Aaron, especially then, in the last two weeks of Angels' existence, when she was planning a climax to all her schemes.

'I need to see you, Karen,' he said, his voice taking on the plaintive whine she despised.

'Really? And are you going to bring the lovely Serena with you?'

'Karen! Look, what are you hiding from me?'

She frowned, concentrating on negotiating a bend in the road before answering him. 'You'll see when you get here,' she snapped. 'It's good for business, though, Aaron,' she told him, her tone softening a little. 'Wait and see – you won't be disappointed!'

She heard his sharp intake of breath and smiled. 'See you in a fortnight!' she said brightly, before breaking the connection and switching the phone to 'off'. There was only one thing for it – Aaron would somehow have to be incorporated into her plans.

It had been a glorious summer so far, but this was the time of day Karen loved best, when the afternoon heat had begun to slide into the balmy cool of the evening, and the beaches were beginning to empty as the tourists went back to their hotels to prepare for dinner.

Maria and Anita were orchestrating Ronan's induction by themselves today. They were, however, also rather preoccupied with each other, and with the novelty of their relationship, and Karen hoped they wouldn't forget their primary purpose in the black room, which was to make sure Ronan was ready for phase two.

Parking opposite one of the main beaches, Karen picked up her bag and walked quickly across the road, and on to the golden sand. The sand had been absorbing the sun's heat all day, and it felt warm between her bare toes as she slipped off her pumps and slung them, their laces tied together, around her neck.

The wide expanse of beach was virtually deserted. To her left, a family were unhurriedly packing away, and beyond them a young couple lay, closely entwined, on the sand. Smiling wryly, Karen guessed that they had probably been like that for most of the day. She envied them their uncomplicated, youthful passion, even while it reminded her uncomfortably of herself, years before. That had been a long time ago – she was virtually a different person now. The thought made her feel unbearably lonely.

Turning away abruptly, she sat down on the sand and spread out her bare legs in front of her, bathing them in the sun. She took too little time to simply sit and be, she thought, dreamily. Since arriving on the island, she had been restless, constantly hyped-up, and her continuing crusade to educate the bar boys who flocked to the resort afforded her little opportunity to really switch off.

If she could teach just one of them to respect the women he slept with, she thought she would have done some good. Men were so stupid. If only they realised how much better for them it would be, how much more satisfying, if they attended lovingly to a woman's needs before their own. A whole new world would open up to them, a whole new world of sensual opportunity . . .

Karen lay back on the warm sand with a sigh. Who was she trying to kid? There was only one man she really wanted to re-educate, and he was beyond redemption.

She dozed lightly, relaxing even while not quite letting go of her awareness of her surrounding. When a shadow passed across the sun, she opened her eyes at once. She struggled into a sitting position, only to find herself being pinned down and pushed on to her back again by a large, strong hand.

'Ricardo! What – '

He cut her off by crushing her mouth under his, his lips hard and uncompromising, his tongue thrusting possessively into her mouth. In spite of herself, Karen felt her body responding, and even revelling in the feeling of his hard, strong frame pressing hers against the sand.

She could feel his heart hammering wildly in his chest and she had to fight the urge to kiss him back. She spent her entire sexual life subjugating the men she met, yet it was this one brutish, domineering bastard who had the power to arouse her, instantly and without mercy.

'What the hell . . .?' she gasped, as he pulled his mouth savagely away from hers.

He allowed her to sit up then, rocking back on his heels, but remaining on his haunches as his dark eyes raked her face.

'What is it about you that means I can't keep my hands off you?' he said, unknowingly echoing her own thoughts.

'No one's forcing you,' she spat, sliding her bottom backward on the sand to put some distance between them.

It made no difference. She could still feel the animal heat of his body, still smell the unique and potent tang of his skin. His happening upon her like this, so unexpectedly as she drowsed, had breached her carefully erected defences. Though she glared indignantly at him, her eyes hard and defiant, she knew that her body betrayed her. His eyes lingered on the rapid rise and fall of her breasts under the flimsy blouse, and she guessed that he sensed her arousal.

'I can't seem to help myself,' he said quietly.

That soft admission affected her far more profoundly than any further show of brute strength could have done. She wanted him with an urgency which took her breath away, and she knew at once that the only way she could regain the upper hand over him was by taking the initiative now.

Holding his eye, she unfastened her shorts and eased them down over her hips, taking her bikini bottoms with them. Oblivious to their exposed position on the beach, she slowly slid her heels apart to reveal the swollen, moisture-slicked folds of flesh between her thighs.

Ricardo swallowed, his Adam's apple bobbing in the slim, brown column of his throat. His eyes were hot, lambent with desire, and his jeans bulged with barely contained passion.

'My God, Karen, you are a whore!' he breathed, viciously.

She ran her fingers down the insides of her thighs until they touched the honeyed well of her vagina. Leaning forward from the waist, she hissed at him. 'If I am a whore, then it was you who made me one.'

'How? When I met you you were a pure, sweet girl.'

'Exactly!'

'It was you who left, you who ran away to follow the path of perversion and dishonour.'

'Oh, *please* – you set yourself up as a saint, Ricardo, yet you are far more of a whore than I with your constant stream of fresh flesh! At least I don't take money from the men I screw!'

'Enough!'

'No, not nearly enough. You – you self-righteous prig! Your eyes flash disgust at me while your body tells me all too clearly that you want me now, just as much as you always have.'

She slipped her forefingers into her moist vagina, scooping up the juices and smearing them across her open labia. Ricardo watched, as if mesmerised, as she teased her clitoris from beneath its protective hood, circling it with her fingertip and scratching gently at its base with her nail.

Watching his face, she masturbated herself, not knowing whether she wanted him to take over, or to walk away. Sweat broke out on Ricardo's brow and his mouth set in a hard, uncompromising line.

'Stop that!' he growled, angrily.

'This is my body,' she jeered, 'to do with as I please. I can make myself come at the touch of a button – ' she pressed lightly against the sensitive tip of her clitoris, sending little sparks of pre-orgasmic pleasure ricocheting through her body. 'I don't need you, Ricardo, not for this, not for anything . . .'

He gave a deep, angry growl as he knocked her hand away and replaced it with his own.

'No?' he said, pinching the small nugget of flesh between his finger and thumb. 'Say you don't need me now!'

Karen moaned as she felt her imminent orgasm ebbing away under the pressure of his cruel fingers.

'I don't need you, Ricardo,' she whispered, against the hot curve of his shoulder.

He entered her with three fingers, scissoring them apart so that she was stretched open, vulnerable to him.

'You are a callous, scheming bitch, Karen, but I'll fuck you all the same.'

She writhed on his fingers as he unfastened his jeans with his free hand. Now pinning her down on to the sand with the upper half of his body, he pushed them down just far enough to allow his cock to spring free.

'Don't you dare!' she warned, close to orgasm again as he rubbed at her burning clit.

Ricardo paused, relaxing his hold on her, calling her bluff. If she protested or resisted now, he would, hugely aroused though he was, take things no further. He stared into her violet eyes; the slightest spark of fear, of uncertainty and he would release her.

Glancing down, Karen could see that the bulb of his cock was only millimetres away from her vagina. She looked up again, narrowing her eyes in defiance as she stared, once again, into his dark brown ones.

Ricardo tilted his hips slightly, so that his cock-tip butted gently against her cunt. Still she said nothing.

'Oh, but I do dare,' he told her through gritted teeth, 'and you will enjoy every minute of it, since I doubt you've had a real man since the last time we fucked.'

'You flatter yourself, Ricardo,' she whispered, determined to make things as difficult as possible for him now that their battle of wills had recommenced. She bucked beneath him.

He thrust hard into her, as though her pleasure was unimportant to him, and yet he managed, unnervingly, to trigger the most delicious responses with every stroke. Karen cried out as her clitoris spasmed and waves of orgasmic heat raced through her, bathing Ricardo's marauding cock with hot, lubricating fluid.

'Tell me you don't need me now,' he growled, his lips against her hair. 'Tell me now how much you hate me!'

'I hate you, Ricardo,' she whispered in anguish, 'I hate you for what you did.'

'Hate me more for what I am about to do,' he said, pulling back her head so that he could see her eyes again. 'For I hate you, Karen, for trying to ruin me and my sister with your schemes and shamelessness. Hate me for this.'

And with that, he withdrew sharply from her and leapt to his feet. She watched with growing incredulity as he forced his erect shaft back into his jeans and, with one last, contemptuous glance at her, he strode purposefully away, leaving her lying sprawled on the sand, aching and empty.

Chapter Nine

*A*rriving back at Angels, Karen was more than ready to take over Ronan's training. The club was buzzing with late-afternoon customers, young women back from the beach, calling in for a drink on the way back to their hotels, where they would change for dinner. Many of them would return afterwards, and Karen acknowledged several who had become regulars for the duration of their holiday.

'Busy tonight, Karen,' Peter remarked, as she passed him.

He shivered ecstatically as she gave him a cold look.

'Did I ask for your opinion?' she said icily.

'No, mistress,' he replied, with relish.

He was older than her usual type, probably in his mid-forties, though his body was still passably firm and his ability to please undiminished. His pale blue eyes watched her hopefully as she considered the fact that he had been granted very few sexual favours since he had arrived four weeks previously, and that since then he had worked for nothing but his bed and board.

Unlike Dale, who had had to return to his desk at the bank after his two week holiday was over, Peter had elected to stay for the duration of their eight-week lease, and Karen recognised that she had been remiss in ignoring him.

'Are you coping with our guests, Peter?' she asked him, in a more kindly tone.

His pale skin flushed as he nodded. 'Yes, mistress. They mainly want no more than a little light hand relief.'

Karen reached forward and ran her thumb across his lower lip. Instantly, he opened his mouth, allowing her access to the sensitive inner flesh.

'Do you tell them your speciality is cunnilingus?' she asked him huskily, making him moan softly.

'No, mistress, but several have found out for themselves without my advertising the fact.'

Karen laughed and withdrew her hand. 'I have a special job for you later. Did you see the new boy, Ronan?'

Peter's eyes lit up – he was quite partial to a taste of male flesh on occasion. 'Yes, mistress.'

'Pretty, isn't he?'

'Indeed.'

'Book a taxi and bring him to the villa after the bar closes tonight – I intend to accelerate his training. I'm in the mood to play tonight.'

Peter nodded and, taking her outstretched hand,

he brought it up to his lips. 'It will be my pleasure, mistress,' he said softly.

Karen fixed him with the steely glance she knew he loved. 'You had better make damn sure, Peter, that it is mine also,' she said frostily, before moving away.

'Ricardo?'

He turned away from the window through which he had been staring morosely, watching the sunset, at the sound of Maria's voice behind him.

'Maria. Why are you here?'

He saw a flash of hurt at his tone pass across her features and he regretted it, but he couldn't bring himself to soften towards her. She had chosen to align herself with Karen, against him, and he could not forgive her for that.

'I've come to collect some more of my things,' she told him, keeping a distance between them. 'I – I've fallen in love, Ricardo, and I'm moving in with my lover.'

Shock kept him immobile.

'Maria – '

'Don't say anything, Ricci,' she pleaded, holding up her hand. 'I don't expect you to understand, and I don't want us to fight.'

Ricardo stared at her, aware that something had changed; there was a kind of glow about her that lit up her lovely face from within. He recognised the look in her eyes; it was the same look that Karen's eyes had used to hold whenever she had looked at him, so long ago. Remembering made him suddenly irritable.

'Who is this man? He shan't get away with dishonouring my sister.

'Ric – '

'Hello, Ricardo.'

Anita appeared at the door, and for a moment he was confused. He hadn't heard anything of her since their last encounter, and he had assumed she had gone home, not sparing her another thought. Then she moved to put a protective arm around Maria's shoulders and, as Maria looked at her with love in her eyes, he realised what was going on.

'God Almighty, Maria, you cannot mean – '

'She does. Don't say anything more, Ricardo, not if you want to salvage something of your sister's love for you.'

'Is that why you are doing this? To punish me for rejecting you?'

Anita shook her head. 'God, Ricardo, you are so conceited! Do you think that once you have slept with a woman everything, her every emotion, is dependent on you? I'm here with Maria because I love her. Obviously, it would make Maria happy if you gave us your blessing, but *I* would settle merely for your silence. Please, for Maria's sake, allow yourself to get used to the idea before you say anything else.'

Ricardo stared at the two women, feeling as though the world had shifted on its axis. He had loved and protected his sister since their father had died when she was ten. He had imagined her settled with a good man and children at her feet, safe and happy. And now this blonde woman

whom he had jilted was telling him that she loved
Maria, that his sister was a lesbian.

'Maria?' he said quizzically.

With a small smile at Anita, she came across the
room and put her arms about him.

'I love you, Ricardo,' she said softly, so that only
he could hear. 'Be happy for me, please?'

He could not give her the reassurance she
wanted: his heart was still too heavy with shock.
He did hold her close for a wordless moment,
though, and he hoped that that was enough to
signal his concern for her.

They left silently, leaving him alone again to
contemplate the sunset. This was Karen's doing, he
was sure of it. A part of him knew he was being
unreasonable, that Maria's sexual orientation could
not have been affected by Karen, or anyone else,
but he clung to his prejudice, needing to feel sure
of his ground.

His love for Karen burned bright in his heart, but
it was tempered by his anger at what she had done.
Stolen his business, corrupted his sister, disturbed
his peace of mind.

As the anger burned slowly through his veins, he
vowed to stop Karen in her tracks. She belonged to
him, why had he not seen that before? They would
marry and she would learn to live the life of a good
wife. In time, this would make her happy, just as it
would make him happy.

He relaxed. That was decided, then. It was time
for him to settle down, and Karen needed a firm
hand. It wasn't natural for a woman to conduct her
life with such blatant disregard for those around

her. He would subdue her, bend her to his will. She wouldn't like it at first, but she would come around to his way of thinking eventually, and then she would thank him for saving her soul.

He would bide his time until Ronan came back to him with information he could use against her. There was something, he was sure of it, some detail that would put her in his hands. He just had to rein in his impatience and wait. She would be his eventually.

Karen lay back in the warm, scented bathwater and closed her eyes. The villa was so peaceful, with only the gentle symphony of the sea outside her window and not a human voice to be heard.

Allowing her hands to drift between her thighs, she touched her fingertips lightly against the swollen bulb of her clitoris. It had been like this since Ricardo had walked away from her on the beach, leaving her angry and frustrated. She was helpless in the face of her passion for him. He was chauvinistic, unreliable, sexually domineering – totally wrong for her. Yet no other man had ever triggered in her such violent yearnings, such an obsessive need.

With a groan, she pressed the heel of her hand down over her mons, feeling the steady pulse beating in her clitoris as she thought of him. In all the years since she had left Tierra del Sol as a heartbroken teenager, she had rarely allowed a man to penetrate her. She sought her pleasures in countless other ways, but sexual intercourse itself held, for her, an intimacy which she did not want to share with anyone else.

When he had sunk into her on the beach that afternoon, she had felt, even more so than when they had first rekindled their sexual relationship at his house, as if she had come home. All these years, and her vagina had indeed retained the memory of the imprint of his cock inside her, possessing her as only he could.

Wouldn't he love to know that he held such power over her! If she could only get him into the black room and break him sexually as she had broken so many others. If she could garner a healthy contempt for him, she was certain that this inconvenient obsession would fade away and die.

Peter and Ronan were due at any moment, so she pulled out the plug and dried herself. Dressing in no more than her red silk kimono, she went to light perfumed candles in the living room before taking a bottle of champagne out of the refrigerator.

Glancing at the clock on the mantelpiece, she put some moody classical music on the CD player she had brought with her from England, before lying down on the sofa, putting her feet up on the arm. It was after midnight; she had expected them to be here by now.

According to Anita, Ronan had almost fainted with shock when he had discovered what they had in store for him in the back room. Ultimately, though, he had enjoyed himself. The girls had strict instructions to release any man who did not give his full consent to their games. So far, though, only one recruit had backed off from making the commitment Karen wanted.

She was pleased with the boys she had trained so far – all of them were popular with the clientele, and Angels had quickly become *the* place to go for women holidaying in groups or alone. Their success had convinced Karen that most women *did* want a holiday fling, but that negative attitudes, such as those displayed by Ricardo and his studs at the Bar del Amore, put them off, made them exercise caution. No woman wanted her name bandied about as a sure bet, or her liaisons taped and rated in the crudest, locker-room terms.

The front door opened and Karen called out to Peter. 'Come on through.'

She smiled at Ronan. There was none of the previous arrogant ebullience about him, and she wondered for a moment if Anita had been a little over-zealous. After all, the girl was merely a fledgling dominatrix, and her main focus of attention was clearly not the men she was given to practise on, but Maria. Karen felt a twinge of guilt at leaving her to her own devices.

'How was your second interview?' she asked him.

He looked at her then, and she saw the lines of strain around his striking green eyes.

'Come and sit here, beside me,' she said, patting the sofa. 'Peter, pour us all a glass of champagne – poor Ronan looks as though he could do with a little fizz.'

She waited while Peter did as he was asked, and then they all sipped at their glasses.

'Was it very hard?' she asked Ronan gently, after a few minutes.

'You might have warned me,' he said and, as he raised his head Karen saw that his expression was one of wonder.

'If I'd tried to tell you this morning that you would enjoy being beaten and humiliated by two women, what would you have said?' she asked him, wryly.

He smiled. 'I'd have thought you were off your head. At first, I was pretty pissed off. I only went along with it because the girls seemed harmless enough at first. I thought I'd humour them so that I could get my reward at the end of it. You know, dressed like that they were, I thought that if I played my cards right – well, you know . . .

'But it was the weirdest thing; once they'd started, something seemed to kind of come over me, this incredible feeling of rightness – I can't explain it, I don't have the words.'

'It's all right, I know,' Karen told him, stroking his thigh.

'There's just one thing I don't understand,' he said after a moment, his eyes tracking the movements of her long fingers as she massaged his leg. 'This morning you said you were going to train me to please women, to really *like* them, is that not so?'

'Yes, that's right.'

'Well, I don't see that there are many women out there who would want to see a guy strung up and whipped in order to get him going, do you get what I'm saying? I don't see how what happened this afternoon can make me a better lover?'

Karen leant forward and kissed him gently on the corner of his mouth.

'It's all about finding out the truth about yourself,' she explained, her fingers describing ever-decreasing circles on his thigh as they edged towards his crotch. 'You see, without self-knowledge it is impossible to give oneself to anything, or anybody. You have to let go of the image you have of yourself, subjugate it to the demands of your body.'

Peter leant forward and unobtrusively refilled their glasses. Ronan ignored him, staring at Karen as if she was revealing something to him of enormous spiritual importance.

'You'll understand tonight's lesson better,' she told him, squeezing the soft bulge at his groin. 'You'll find it more relevant.'

Karen signalled to Peter and waited while he helped Ronan out of his clothes.

'You have a wonderful body, Ronan,' she said, eyeing his long, pale limbs appreciatively. 'Don't you think so, Peter?'

'Indeed, mistress,' Peter said, brushing his fingertips across the breadth of Ronan's shoulders.

Ronan flinched, darting an anxious look at Karen. 'I'm not ... like that,' he told her urgently, clearly terrified by the prospect of Peter trying to take things further.

Karen smiled reassuringly at him. 'Ronan,' she said, 'let me assure you that you will never be expected to do anything that you don't truly want to do. All that I ask is that you keep yourself open to new ideas, new challenges, to let go of your own, restricted view of yourself. Deal?'

'But I'm not a homosexual,' he pressed.

Karen shrugged. 'That's just a label, like "tall", or "fine-boned". You would never say "I'm not hungry" with such an air of permanence, would you? In an hour or two you might well be.'

She could see that she had confused him, so she reached for his flaccid penis. It swelled immediately at her touch, and she stroked the soft skin which enclosed the iron core of his shaft, drawing him closer to her.

'I want you to kneel, Ronan, and then I want you to make me come, using only your lips and tongue. Peter?'

Peter tied a silk scarf he had ready around Ronan's wrists, fastening them at the small of his back.

'This time, the bondage is just to help you obey my instruction. In time, it won't be needed at all,' she explained kindly.

Ronan sank to his knees and, although the anxious expression had not entirely gone, he looked more comfortable now that he had been told his task for the evening.

Slowly, watching his face, Karen parted the two sides of her silk kimono, to reveal the well-groomed triangle of dark hair at the apex of her thighs. Seeing how the perspiration broke out over his top lip, she lifted one leg up on to the sofa and parted her labia with her fingers.

'Come,' she whispered.

Ronan bent his head, touching his tongue against her exposed clitoris with a muffled sigh.

'Not too rough, take it gently – that's it, long, slow strokes. Savour the experience,' she said, making herself more comfortable against the cushions. 'I intend to.'

At her signal, Peter came over and kissed her lingeringly on the lips. She sighed as Ronan began to lap gently at the stretched membranes between her anus and vagina, then moved upward, the tip of his tongue boring into the moist hole and dragging its secretions up over her labia.

Karen guessed that the girls had jumped forward a step that afternoon, and she made a mental note to tell them not to go so fast. She wasn't complaining, though: at least Ronan had acquired sufficient skill to cause a warm, liquid heat to roll through her veins, making her feel languid and heavy-limbed.

Peter reached down to caress her breasts and she closed her eyes, giving herself over to the sensations. She felt like a queen being pleasured by her courtiers – the ultimate in passive sex. An image of Ricardo as he had looked earlier on the beach pushed its way into her mind, and she felt her intimate flesh convulse against Ronan's lips.

Feeling the change in her, Ronan licked delicately at the base of her clitoris, teasing it until the tremors began, then he flicked it with the very tip of his tongue, strumming it back and forth as Karen gasped and sighed.

When he felt her orgasm beginning to ebb away, he sat back on his heels and gazed at her hopefully.

'Well done,' she said, when she had recovered her breath. 'A little quick, but you seem to have learnt a lot already.'

He smiled, pleased with her praise. His long limbs looked excessively vulnerable in the flickering candlelight and Karen was moved to stroke a hand along his thigh. His penis was stiff and swollen, and she enclosed it in her cool palm, squeezing it gently and rhythmically as he waited passively for her instructions.

'Would you like to come, Ronan?' she asked softly.

'Yes,' he admitted. All afternoon, he had been stimulated beyond the bounds of his control, and not once had he been offered any relief. Maria, Anita, and now Karen had all pushed him to his limits, using him for their own pleasure, but Karen had been the first to acknowledge that he had needs of his own. He waited silently and patiently, hoping she might allow him access to the lush, fragrant body he had just tasted. Her next words, however, chilled him.

'I will allow you to come, Ronan,' she said, 'but you are to shoot your seed down Peter's throat.'

'I – I can't!' he cried, anguished at the very thought of what she wanted him to do.

Karen leant forward and clasped his face between her hands. He found himself drowning in the deep violet colour of her eyes, and his head began to spin.

'Do it,' she whispered urgently. 'Do it for me.'

Lost for words, he rose to his feet and waited passively for Peter to kneel in front of him. He closed his eyes at the first touch of Peter's mouth against his glans. Ricardo would have to pay him one hell of a lot extra for this final indignity, he vowed to himself.

'Relax, Ronan,' Karen said. Her voice seemed to come from far away, even though she was only on the sofa in front of him. 'If you really did object so much, don't you think your erection would have disappeared by now?'

Opening his eyes, he looked down to see his stiff rod moving back and forth between Peter's lips. It showed no sign of softening, or of shrinking away in disgust as he felt it should. The shame of it! He stifled a groan of abject humiliation whilst at the same time moving his hips so that his penis drove more deeply in to the other man's mouth.

'That's right, my love,' Karen said, her voice low and hypnotic, 'use his mouth, then later, if you're really good, we'll let him have your arse.'

Her words spurred him on, making his climax inevitable. As his seed rushed along his shaft, and then exploded into Peter's hot mouth, Ronan cried out, not knowing who he was any more. All his former certainty had been stripped away, leaving him bare and vulnerable: a slave to Karen's every whim.

Later, when Peter and Ronan had showered and dressed and shared a second bottle of champagne with her, Karen asked softly, 'When are you due to report back to Ricardo Baddeiras, Ronan?'

His eyes widened guiltily. One look from her warned him not to lie.

'How did you know?' he asked her, his heart hammering wildly in his chest.

'I didn't know for certain, not until you confirmed it just now. But I had my suspicions. I know Señor Baddeiras of old. So, Ricardo has put a spy in our midst. What does he hope to discover, I wonder?'

It was as if, now that the truth was out, Ronan was at pains to make it up to her for his attempted deceit.

'He wanted to find out why his customers were defecting to Angels,' he said, the words tumbling over each other in his rush to get them out. 'He wanted to know why you were trying to put him out of business.'

'I suppose you've already told him we only have four weeks left?'

Ronan nodded, watching her face anxiously, as if he expected some kind of retribution for his transgression.

'I see. Well, I want you to report back as planned – he mustn't suspect that I know that you are working for him.'

'You mean ... like a double agent?' he asked, almost hopefully.

Karen laughed. 'Hardly. I have to decide, though, how best to use you. Take him back to Angels, Peter, and stay in his room tonight.' She did not miss the apprehensive glance that Ronan gave Peter, but she did not bother to reassure him. He'd find out soon enough that Peter would make no move on him unless specifically requested to do so by her. 'We'll talk in the morning,' she said.

Both men kissed her goodnight, but her mind had already moved on, and she was distracted as they said their goodbyes. It was time, she decided, to evict Ricardo from that corner of her mind, from which he dominated her every thought and deed. Time to let him know once and for all that he had no claim on her. All she had to do now was work out how the hell she was going to manage it.

Her mobile phone rang and she picked it up with a frown. It was Aaron.

'I can't wait for two weeks,' he said, without any preliminary greeting.

'What are you talking about?'

'Speaking to you this afternoon – it's been too long, Karen. I'm flying out tomorrow, I'll be with you by six o'clock, your time. Could you pick me up at the airport?'

She battened down her fury, knowing that he had made up his mind, and that again there was nothing she could say to make him change his plans.

'It's very inconvenient,' she told him, as she knew he would expect her to.

'I want to see my investment, Karen: I want to see how you have been spending my money.'

She sighed theatrically, though her exasperation was not altogether feigned. Having Aaron around would severely cramp her style, especially when it came to dealing with Ricardo.

'Very well,' she said, 'I'll meet your plane tomorrow. But you're going to have to pay for this, Aaron, do you understand?'

'Of course – don't we always understand each other?' he said.

Karen pursed her lips, irritated by his presumption. He always tried to resist her subjugation of him, fighting her every inch of the way. It was why their relationship had lasted longer than most.

'Bring something with which I can chastise you,' she instructed. 'Something small and relatively discreet, so that you don't get stopped at customs.'

She could hear the quickening of Aaron's breath as he listened to her, but she didn't wait for his reply. Cutting the connection, she switched the phone off altogether and went to get some sleep. Tomorrow was going to be a long day.

The news reached Maria by way of a hand-written note, at mid-morning the following day.

'Maria? What is it?' Anita asked, seeing the other girl's shock.

Maria lifted dark eyes, which already were swimming with tears to look at her friend.

'My uncle, Julio Escobar. He died last night.'

'Oh, baby!' Anita hugged her, stroking her hair. 'What do you need to do? Can I help?'

Maria dried her eyes and thought for a moment. 'I must get in touch with Ricardo. He and Julio did not get on, but he will want to pay his respects at his funeral tomorrow. And I will need to speak to Julio's lawyer – he always told me to do that, as soon as I heard of his death – ' she broke down and began to weep.

How could he be gone? The last time she had seen him, he had not seemed unduly unwell.

207

'He told me not to come again when I saw him last,' she sobbed into Anita's shoulder. 'He must have known, then. Poor old man – he was all alone apart from that dreadful woman who kept house for him. She doesn't have a gentle bone in her body, what comfort could she have been to him? I should have been there, Anita, I should have *known*. If only I had kept in touch – oh, Uncle Julio Escobar, I am so sorry!'

Anita held Maria while she cried, knowing there was nothing she could do but be there for her. When at last the storm had passed, she handed her a tissue and waited for her to compose herself.

'Do you want me to come with you to see Ricardo?' she asked.

There had been no communication between brother and sister since Maria had visited the house the day before, and Anita was afraid that the girl might have to face outright rejection from him. Nevertheless, she had to admit to feeling relieved when Maria shook her head.

'I can deal with Ricardo,' she promised.

Anita nodded. 'Good girl,' she said softly.

'But you – '

'Go and do what you have to do,' Anita said, anticipating Maria's concern. 'Don't worry about me. I'm sure Karen will keep me busy!'

Maria kissed her and went to get ready.

Ricardo was in the back room at the Bar del Amore, running through the dismal figures for the past month. He looked up to see Maria standing in the doorway, and scowled.

'Have you come to gloat now I am having to lay off staff?' he asked, viciously.

'Ricardo, how can you think such a thing?' She came into the room and sat down in the chair opposite him.

'How are you?' he asked, grudgingly.

'Fine.'

'You look very well.'

'Thank you. You look dreadful.'

'Thank *you*,' he replied with a grim smile.

He gazed at Maria across the desk and, suddenly, it was as if he couldn't keep his feelings in check for a moment longer.

'Just tell me why, Maria, *why* is she doing this to me?'

Maria shook her head and her dark curls moved softly over her cheeks.

'Because she loved you, and you let her down.'

'That was a long time ago. I was young and foolish and I didn't realise what I had.'

Maria wanted to throw her arms around his neck and hug him to her.

'That is the most honest thing you have said to me in years, Ricardo. Have you told Karen this?'

'Of course not!'

'Why not? She might forgive you if she believed that you were sorry.'

Ricardo made an impatient gesture with one hand. He wasn't used to talking about his feelings, and doing so now made him feel intensely uncomfortable.

'Of course I am sorry – Karen must know this.'

'Why would she? She has come back to Tierra del

Sol ten years later, to find you chasing women as if your life depends upon it. What possible reason could she have for suspecting that you have changed? If indeed, you have changed at all.'

'You doubt me?'

'I *know* you, Ricardo.'

Ricardo stared at Maria across the desk and realised, at last, that his little sister had grown up.

'When did you get to be so wise, little one?' he asked softly.

She made a face at him, happy that some of their old, easy camaraderie had been restored. 'I always have been – you've just never taken any notice before!' She became serious again. 'Why don't you talk to her, Ricardo?'

He scowled. 'Why should I?'

Maria leant forward and covered his hand with hers. 'Because you are in love with her, Ricardo. Because I believe that she is in love with you. Make it right between you, before it is too late.'

Ricardo shook his head. 'It is already too late. But you didn't come here to tell me this. Why did you come, Maria?'

Maria sighed. She'd done what she could, and now it was up to Ricardo and Karen to decide whether or not they wanted to sort out their differences. Taking her lead from Ricardo, she changed the subject and told him about Escobar.

Anita found Karen in the bar of Angels, making notes in a purple silk-bound notebook. 'Everyone is sad today,' she said, catching sight of Karen's expression. 'It must be something in the air.' She told Karen about Maria's bereavement, and asked if there was anything she could do while Maria was out.

'There is, actually. The man who put up the money for this place is arriving at six o'clock tonight. He's expecting me to meet him at the airport.'

'Is that a problem?' Anita asked.

Karen looked speculatively at her. Over the past few weeks, she had had something of a crash course in domination. Was she up to containing Aaron for her? Karen decided to take a chance.

'Look, Anita, I know this thing between you and Maria is very new, and that you're both still at the not-wanting-to-be-separated-for-a-minute stage, but I guess Maria will be tied up for the next few days with her uncle's funeral, am I right?'

'I suppose so.'

'Then perhaps you would like to help me with a plan I have?'

Karen outlined the bare bones of her idea to Anita, and they set a date for one week hence.

'I need to get Aaron to agree fully to it. After what we've seen we can do, Angels could become an international concern: we could open up bars in every country in the world. The trouble is that initially, I'll need Aaron's financial input. When he gets off that plane, he's going to expect to see me. He won't be best pleased when you turn up instead.'

'I'll handle him,' Anita said, with a gleam in her eye. 'It'll give me a chance to practise, to hone my skills.'

Karen laughed. 'Darling, you're a natural! But, I admit, practice never goes amiss. I'll go back to the villa and pick up my things. I'll stay here, above the bar until the big night, and you keep Aaron under wraps at the villa. By the time he sees me, he'll be so desperate for me he'll do anything – anything at all.'

'Leave it to me,' Anita said, confidently. 'I'll have him eating out of the palms of our hands.'

The two women shook hands.

'It's going to be a night to remember, Anita. Tierra del Sol will be talking about this for months to come.'

'*Years* to come,' Anita corrected her. 'Men all over the world will hear the name "Angels" and quake in their Calvin Kleins!'

Karen laughed. Anita was right, what they were planning would make waves. So why did she feel so bloody miserable?

Chapter Ten

*R*icardo looked around the deserted bar and set his jaw angrily. It had been like this every night now for a week. Gunter, Jamie and Darren, the only three members of his staff he hadn't let go, sat at the bar, drinking and wearing their boredom like a shroud.

'For the love of God!' Ricardo exploded.

Striding over to the door, he glared at Angels, which as usual, was packed with female revellers. The bright disco lights spilled out on to the pavement, and music blared out through the open windows. There would be complaints from the residents of Leventos before long, he thought sourly. And not before time.

'Has anyone seen Ronan this week?' he asked, turning back to the gloomy interior of his own bar.

They all shook their heads. The day after Maria had come bearing the news about Escobar, Ronan had met Ricardo and had reported that he was still trying to work his way into the women's confidence. He had shrugged when Ricardo had suggested that his report told him nothing, and he had, Baddeiras realised now, also failed to make eye contact at any time during the short meeting.

'This is ridiculous – he can't just have disappeared!'

'Maybe they're driving their staff out into the hills and shooting them,' Jamie suggested, half-heartedly.

'Or keeping them tied to the bed, and forcing them to service every woman who comes their way!' Gunter said, warming to the theme and waggling his tongue obscenely.

Ricardo laughed with the rest, but he felt uneasy. Something was going on, he felt it in his bones.

'Seriously, mate, there have been rumours,' Jamie said, keeping his eyes firmly fixed on his beer glass.

Ricardo frowned. 'Rumours? What kind of rumours?'

Jamie looked uncomfortable. It wasn't easy to be frank with Ricardo when everyone knew that the little sister he adored was involved. 'Apparently, the women who go there are like animals,' he ventured.

'Yes, I have heard this too – no man is safe in Angels,' Gunter said, laughing.

'Don't be absurd!' Ricardo snapped.

'What about Ronan, Ric?' Jamie said seriously. 'No one's seen him now for a week. Then there was that English bloke whose photograph was in the paper – he's been missing for even longer.'

Ricardo picked up the folded newspaper and frowned at the photograph.

'Adrian Brown.' He read the caption underneath and shook his head. 'Why would Angels be involved?'

'Because hours before he disappeared, he was seen talking to an Englishwoman with short black hair,' Jamie said.

'Karen?'

Jamie shrugged. 'Could be.'

'Have you seen these, boss?'

Ricardo turned as Darren spoke, to see him unrolling a glossy poster. It was bright and well-produced, and advertised a 'speciality night' at Angels, due to take place the following evening. The illustration showed a man's bare buttocks, framed by a series of studded black leather straps which spanned his waist and thighs. His white skin was striped with a single pink line, below which lay the shadow of a whip. AVENGING ANGELS ran the caption, FOR THE NIGHT OF YOUR LIFE.

'What is this?' Ricardo said, flicking his fingers against the poster. 'A "speciality night"?'

The men all shrugged their shoulders as he glanced at them. He looked over his shoulder at the bar across the street and frowned.

'Gunter, you go over and see if you can find out anything.'

'But Maria knows me, Ricardo – '

'Maria is out of town, making an inventory of her new property,' he snapped. 'Go over there and pretend I've sacked you, like I had to sack the others. Try to persuade them that you need a job.'

215

'OK,' Gunter said uneasily, 'if that's what you want.'

'Get going.'

Ricardo watched as Gunter slid reluctantly off his bar stool and walked to the door. All his cheerful bravado seemed to have fled now that he was required to do something himself. He glanced back over his shoulder as he reached it, looking like a man on his ways to the gallows.

'Be back here before closing time,' Ricardo warned him.

Gunter left and Ricardo glanced at Jamie and Darren. They were both looking at him as if he had grown horns.

'What?' he snapped, exasperated with them.

'I hope he comes back,' Jamie muttered, turning back to his pint.

'Of course he'll come back!' Ricardo roared, thoroughly agitated. 'For God's sake, we know the women who run this bar – Maria, Karen, Anita.'

'Exactly,' Darren said cryptically.

Ricardo threw up his hands in despair. 'You're acting like a pair of hysterical old women! He'll come back,' he repeated.

He didn't. Ricardo gave up waiting and closed the bar when Gunter hadn't reappeared by 3 a.m. When Jamie and Darren reported for work at lunchtime the following day, he shrugged his shoulders, at a loss for an explanation.

'He probably got lucky,' he said.

Jamie and Darren looked at each other significantly.

'Nothing has happened to Gunter,' said Ricardo. 'Look, if it makes you feel better, you can go and fetch him tonight.'

Darren shook his head. 'No way am I setting foot in that bar,' he said.

'Me neither,' Jamie piped up.

Ricardo looked from one to the other of them in disbelief. 'Just what *do* you think is going on over there?' he asked, sarcastically.

Darren gave him a level look. 'Female things,' he said darkly.

'Witchcraft,' Jamie added, clearly having discussed the whole thing with Darren.

Ricardo shook his head. 'You two are unbelievable. I say Gunter is probably at this very moment having the time of his life. You know what he's like – he's a quick-fuck merchant, one woman after another.'

They still didn't look convinced, and he rolled his eyes heavenward. 'OK, I'll make a deal with you. We'll wait until after this "speciality night" has begun. He would hardly hang around for that, would he? If he's not back by then, *I'll* go and look for him.'

Jamie and Darren looked alarmed. 'I don't think you should, boss,' Darren said, clearly uncomfortable with the idea.

'Then what do you suggest?'

'We should all go,' Jamie said. 'We'll give it until ten, and then we'll all go over and find out what's going on.'

'Safety in numbers,' Darren agreed.

Ricardo shook his head. 'I can't believe you two

217

are that afraid of a bunch of troublesome women,'
he said contemptuously, 'but if it makes you feel
happier, then I agree. Ten o'clock it is – and we all
go together.'

Karen, Maria and Anita took their time in getting
ready. In keeping with her more submissive inclination, Maria was wearing a floaty, white chiffon
dress with a large, flounced all-round collar and
flowing sleeves. It would have looked very feminine and demure had it not been for the fact that it
was diaphanous, totally see-through, and she was
not wearing any underwear.

Anita made her parade up and down the dressing
room, and watched her large, brown-tipped breasts
bounce, catching tempting glimpses of the dark
triangle of hair between her thighs as she moved.
Then she pulled her into her arms.

'You look wonderful, darling,' she said fervently,
kissing Maria on the lips.

Karen watched them with mild amusement. 'I
know you two have been apart for a whole week,
but can you *please* try to concentrate on the job in
hand? I can't run the whole show on my own!'

They broke apart regretfully.

'Sorry, Karen,' Anita said, patting Maria on the
bottom before moving resolutely away from her.

'Well, I can hardly complain, can I?' Karen said,
smiling at Maria as she spoke to Anita. 'You managed to keep Aaron out of my hair. How's he been?'

Anita grinned.

'Good as gold. I'll admit I overstepped the mark

a bit at first, but he didn't seem to mind. No serious damage,' she said cheerfully.

Karen resisted the urge to ask her to elaborate – so long as Aaron was happy, she wasn't going to interfere.

'Does he know we're going to make him a star?' Karen asked, sardonically.

'Yes. I had to make him promises though, to get him to agree.'

'Promises?' Karen and Maria said together.

Anita's cheeks pinkened.

'Yes. You see, he likes – well, he likes me to piss on him.'

'What?' Maria cried, horrified.

'I know – you wouldn't credit it, would you? Only, you see, Karen, I had to promise that I'd do it onstage, tonight as a kind of climax. Do you think maybe that'll be a bit strong for the audience?'

Karen shook her head. Trust Aaron to make life complicated! 'Play it by ear. If you can get him so worked up that he's pleading for you to do it, you might find the women will egg you on, then it'd be okay, I guess.'

She and Anita were wearing identical black leather basques and lace-up, thigh-high boots. Karen had elected to wear shiny black PVC briefs, while Anita had shaved her pussy especially for the occasion, and was proud to display it publicly. Her inner labia protruded temptingly from between the outer lips, their surface pink and smooth in contrast to the white skin of her pubis. The hood of her clitoris was just visible at the apex of her labia, and

Karen guessed that she was already aroused, ready to begin.

There was a light tap on the door and Peter slipped in through it.

'Yes? What is it?' Karen said.

'Excuse, me, mistress, but I thought you might like to know that we've had to close the doors – we're full to capacity.'

'Good. Well, Peter? Why are you still here?'

The wretched man wrung his hands, and at that moment he looked every inch a total wimp. 'They seem very rowdy, mistress,' he said.

Karen sighed. 'Peter, if it gets too much for you, you have my permission to lock yourself in my office.'

'Oh, thank you, mistress, you are too kind.'

'Yes, I probably am. Leave us – and check on the men, particularly the new one. Make sure none of them bottle out and make a sudden bolt for it.'

'Yes, mistress,' he said, backing out of the room, the picture of subservience.

Karen stood up and smiled at her co-conspirators. 'Are you ready, ladies?' she asked softly.

Maria looked apprehensive, but there was a gleam in Anita's eye to which she could relate.

'One last thing.' Karen reached into a box and brought out three exquisitely embroidered eye masks. Maria's was white, to match her outfit, and trimmed with swansdown. When she had put it on, she looked like Odile from *Swan Lake*, beautiful and untouchable.

'Charming,' Karen said, kissing her softly on the cheek.

220

Anita's mask was very similar in style to Maria's, but it was black and trimmed with black marabou feathers which framed her face. Karen's glittered with tiny jet beads which tinkled slightly as she moved.

As one, the three women turned to look at themselves in the mirror.

'We look magnificent!' Anita breathed, awed by her own reflection.

Karen smiled. 'We *are* magnificent,' she said, taking both their hands and giving them a squeeze. 'We are the Avenging Angels – all for one and one for all!'

Laughing, they embraced before turning for the door.

Peter was right – it was a rowdy crowd. For fifty pounds a head, the audience expected something spectacular, and Karen sensed that a significant number were preparing themselves to be disappointed. The atmosphere was not the usual friendly one, and Karen braced herself to turn it around.

'Ladies,' she said, striding out on to the stage and calling for their attention. She waited until they had quietened down, adopting an aggressive stance, legs apart, hands firmly placed on her hips. Gradually, everyone turned towards her. She could feel their eyes taking in her outlandish outfit, and sensed their surprise – and anticipation.

'Ladies, I'd like to welcome you to Angels, and to introduce you to the participants in tonight's show. Peter?'

She turned and signalled for Peter to bring on the

first man. A gasp went up from the assembled crowd as Adrian shuffled on to the stage. His wrists and ankles were manacled together with heavy chains, making it impossible for him to move quickly. He was naked save for a pair of black rubber boxer shorts, stretched tight to delineate the straight, erect line of his penis. His dark blond head was bowed, and his eyes lowered, as he took his place at the centre of the stage.

'Ladies, this is Adrian. Adrian has been trained by us for a good few weeks now, and I can guarantee he'll give you satisfaction. Isn't that so, Adrian?'

Adrian raised his head and looked proudly around the room at the assembled women, most of whom had stopped their discontented mumbling and were gazing in awe at the sight presented to them. His eyes were bright and he glanced at Karen with a look of pure adoration on his face.

'I aim to please, mistress,' he said, loudly and clearly for all to hear.

The women went wild, whooping and cheering as Karen led Adrian to one side of the stage, where Anita was waiting for him. Assisted by Maria, she unfastened his chains, then strapped him to the square wooden frame erected especially for the occasion. This had been mounted on a podium which swivelled through 180° at the pull of a lever, and at each of its corners was attached a metal ring, which gleamed under the stage lights.

Adrian positioned himself happily. His arms were outstretched, his legs apart, far enough to make him vulnerable, but close enough together to allow him to stay in the same position in relative comfort for perhaps an hour or more. As Anita fastened leather cuffs around his wrists and ankles and secured him to the metal rings, a beatific expression spread across his face, as if he was about to undergo a spiritual experience.

Using the props Karen had carefully set up to act as a trigger for him, Maria began to rub his torso with oil until his skin shone under the spotlight. The simple massage was enough to make his already turgid cock swell significantly in his tight rubber boxers, much to the delight of the audience.

'Later on, ladies, we'll be running a contest to pick a member of the audience to help Anita and Maria to relieve Adrian of his – ' she cleared her throat ' – his considerable burden,' Karen said, laughing as Anita flicked a light fly-whip across the sharply outlined shaft, causing the tight fabric to stretch dangerously thin as his cock swelled still more.

Adrian closed his eyes momentarily and swallowed hard, trying to control his body's reaction to the deliberate baiting. Karen smiled approvingly at him when he opened his eyes. He had learned his every lesson well, even begging her not to make him leave when he was reported missing. Karen had made him contact the police and his family to reassure them that he was all right, and she hoped that no more would come of it.

A roar went up as Peter led on the next participant. Karen turned and again smiled approvingly as Ronan dropped to his knees at her feet and bent forward to press his lips against the sharply pointed toe of her boot.

He was naked saved for a series of leather straps, decorated with silver studs. The thickest was fastened around his waist and from either side of it, two split straps formed a triangle, similar to suspenders, which were attached to thinner straps around each of his thighs. His slender cock was restrained by a soft, suedette pouch dyed silver and decorated with fronds of silver thread.

'Meet Ronan,' Karen said, pausing to stroke his dark, silky hair as he pressed his lips against the tops of her boots, halfway up her thighs. 'Ronan wants to share his sexual liberation with you – Peter?'

Peter stepped forward eagerly, and handed Karen a tube of lubricant. Concentrating on the man who was trembling at her feet, Karen ignored the lewd remarks being made by the audience as she leant over him and began to work the thick, sticky gel along the crease between Ronan's buttocks and around his anal sphincter.

This had been Ronan's own idea. Days of careful desensitisation had put him in touch with his darkest fantasies, making him yearn for the homosexual encounter which he had always craved, albeit subconsciously. And now he was going to experience the penetration of his virgin hole in full view of an audience of women. Karen knew that the humiliation would add to the experience a piquancy that he would never be able to forget, an erotic charge which he would recall again and again in the years to come.

'Hush now,' she murmured as she felt him trembling.

Crouching down in front of him, she stroked his face. He looked up at her with his clear green eyes and she saw that they looked very large in his white face.

'Would you like to leave?' she asked him gently.

A look of panic passed across his pretty features.

'No! Please, don't make me go. Let me stay, like we said . . .?'

Karen smiled kindly at him, and bent to kiss his soft lips. They trembled deliciously beneath hers and for a moment she wished the audience would melt away so that she could have him to herself. These same lips had learnt to work miracles in the moist, silky recesses of her most intimate flesh . . .

'Very well,' she said briskly, standing up again. 'Go and take your place beside Adrian.'

While Ronan scrambled to do her bidding, the audience let out a collective gasp of mingled shock and excitement as they saw the next participant. Aaron was clothed from head to foot in shiny black PVC. His head was covered by a tight-fitting hood with two small holes cut for his nostrils and a slit for his mouth. His eyes and ears were completely covered and Karen knew that his senses would be muted, the sounds around him subdued to a low murmur as he was led to the centre of the stage.

Karen knew he would be able to smell the excitement in the room – it rose up from the audience like a thick miasma, a combination of perfume, fresh perspiration and feminine arousal. The fact that he could not see the women would make the excitement all the more acute for Aaron, for his imagination was such that it would conjure up scenes of degradation far worse than the one to which he was about to be subjected.

His bodysuit covered his hands and feet, but there was a hole at his crotch which left his penis hanging free. It looked very white against the unrelenting glossy black of the PVC, very vulnerable. Nevertheless, the moment Karen touched it with her crop, it engorged with blood and rose like an angry red sentinel, pointing directly at the audience.

'Ooh! Don't you point that thing at me!' someone shouted.

'It might go off!' her friend shrieked, collapsing into a fit of the giggles.

Karen could feel the tension in Aaron's limbs and knew that he was relishing every moment of this abject humiliation. She shook her head in wonder at the depth of his need for debasement. Touching his shoulder, she turned him around to display the holes cut strategically in the rear of his bodysuit.

His buttocks, too, were white, and almost luminous in the harsh glare of the spotlight. Karen slapped him several times to bring some colour to his cheeks.

The crowd went wild, stamping their feet and cheering. Karen watched them and smiled. How many women out there had long harboured a secret desire to dominate and control their men like this? How many were natural dominatrixes, suppressing their instincts to conform to society's narrow, constricting view of what a woman should be – inside the bedroom and out of it?

Karen felt a rush of adrenalin as she guided Aaron to stand in line with Ronan, who was still on his knees, and Adrian, strapped to his wooden frame. She beckoned to Peter. The fourth and final man came into the spotlight reluctantly, his head bowed and his dark blond hair falling in a concealing curtain over his gaunt cheeks. Though his torso was naked, he was wearing his jeans, albeit unfastened, the button fly flapping open to reveal a thick nest of pubic hair curling over the surrounding denim.

She felt a twinge of unease. He looked disorientated, startled by the mass of women all leering up at him, and she feared that Anita might not have obtained the full and free consent needed from him for him to take part in the show they had planned.

Approaching him, she lifted his face between her two hands and said quietly, 'Are you all right?'

His eyes looked unfocused, but there was a dawning light in them that reassured her. He was simply dazed, confused by the speed at which events had overtaken him.

Karen ran her palms across his bare torso, allowing her fingers to linger on his nipples, playing with the gold rings he had pierced through them. She signalled to Peter, took the fine chain he handed her, and held it up so that the audience could see that it split into two halfway along. At the end of each split half was a clip. Attaching the clips to the nipple rings, she slung the long chain over her shoulder and, turning her back on him, paraded him to the centre of the stage.

For Karen, this was going to be the most satisfying display of all. This man was the reason she had been sent to Tierra del Sol in the first place: without his misdemeanours, she might never have returned. Now she had him completely at her mercy and she felt a swift, sharp dart of lust to her loins.

Raking the audience with her gaze, she saw that any hostility which might have coloured proceedings at first had now dissipated, swept aside by a rampaging surge of female hormones. She was sure that there wasn't a woman in the place who didn't wish herself in Karen's boots at that moment, and she revelled in the power surge that thought gave her.

'Many of you will know our final participant, since he's very free with his favours – aren't you, darling?'

She gave a small tug on the gold chain to indicate that she expected him to reply.

'Uh, oh, yes,' he said, his voice cracking with the strain.

'You like the ladies, don't you, Gunter?'

'Very much.' He grinned. 'The ladies, they like me too,' he ventured.

'Tonight we are going to show you what the ladies really want – isn't that right, girls?'

The audience let out an almighty roar, a sound which, to Karen's delight, could by no stretch of the imagination be described as 'ladylike'.

'Then let's begin,' she said, turning to nod at Anita, a wide grin splitting her face.

* * *

Ricardo glanced at his watch. Ten o'clock and still no sign of Gunter. Loud yells and whoops travelled on the warm evening air from the bar opposite, each one fuelling his anger. The Bar del Amore was empty save for Jamie, Darren, old Pedro and himself, as it had been all day.

'Come on,' he said at last. 'We're going over there.'

Jamie and Darren exchanged apprehensive glances, but neither wanted to cross Ricardo while he was in this mood. Already, he was striding out of the bar and across the street towards Angels.

'Can you hold the fort 'til we get back, Pedro?' Darren said, glancing dubiously at the half-blind old man.

'Yes, yes,' he assured them, waving them away with arthritic hands. 'I've been serving drinks since before your fathers were born.' He felt his way around the counter of the bar and took up his position, scowling fiercely. 'You think I can't manage all these people?' he asked, looking around the empty bar.

Darren shrugged and hurried after Ricardo with Jamie reluctantly bringing up the rear.

Ricardo paused as they reached the other side of the street, and regarded Escobar's old bar with a frown. Whatever was going on in there, it was certainly rowdy. If Karen wasn't careful, she'd have the local police nosing around, and that wouldn't be good for business.

He smiled grimly. Maybe he should bring them himself. He knew the officer on duty in Leventos, which was why he had been able to limit the damage Karen had inflicted upon his business when she had first arrived, and it would be simple enough to persuade him to close her down. For some reason, though, he had always baulked at that solution. Whether it was due to a lingering softness towards Karen, or whether he simply couldn't bring himself to have his sister publicly disgraced, he did not know, and cared less to analyse.

Anyway, it wouldn't do, he reasoned, as he signalled to the others to follow him around to the back, for his future wife to have a police record. That might eventually reflect on his own business standing on the island.

As he had suspected, there was no security on the back door, and it was a simple enough matter to slip inside unobserved. Both Darren and Jamie were as jumpy as cat burglars under security flares, and he scowled at them, beckoning them to stay close.

They followed the sounds of merriment coming from the main part of the building. As they passed along the narrow corridor which led from the rear door, Jamie opened a door leading off it and flicked on the light.

'Jesus wept!' he gasped.

Irritated by the diversion, Ricardo nevertheless paused to look inside. His eyes widened as he took in the black-painted walls and the various pieces of equipment which lined them.

The three men looked at each other. There was a gleam in Darren's eye which made Ricardo frown.

'Come on,' Ricardo said, setting his jaw. 'Let's find out what's going on, once and for all.'

At the end of the corridor were two doors, one marked STAGE, the other unmarked. Ricardo opened the stage door quietly, guessing that this was the point from which they would best be able to see the whole of the bar without being observed in their turn. He hadn't expected there to be anything taking place on the stage itself.

The first thing that struck him as he opened the door was a wave of sound, the like of which he had never heard before. A cacophony of female voices, joined as one, was shouting obscenities and encouragement. The heat was incredible, the sickly-sweet smell of perfume overwhelming.

As his eyes adjusted to the bright light, he saw Maria kneeling at the feet of a tall young man whom he felt he ought to recognise.

'Isn't that the guy who was in the paper?' Jamie said, inadvertently echoing his thoughts.

The man was spreadeagled against a wooden frame, and Maria was holding his erect penis, pointing it towards a smartly dressed young woman who had bared her breasts. Anita was bending over her, rubbing oil into the generous globes of flesh, in preparation for the slip of the man's penis across her skin.

Next to them, a man dressed from top to toe in shiny black stood motionless, his hooded head cocked in an attitude of extreme concentration. His naked penis was iron-hard, and glowing red as if it had been on the receiving end of a lot of attention, much to the amusement of the women in the audience.

Ricardo suddenly recognised Ronan, who was

231

crouching on all fours. An older, uknown man was kneeling behind him, his erect cock poised at the forbidden portal to the young Irishman's body. Ronan's face was turned towards the man, watching him over his shoulder, and his expression was an emotive mix of excitement and terror.

As Ricardo watched in horrified fascination, the unknown man eased himself into Ronan's anus. An unholy cheer went up from the female audience as Ronan collapsed forward on to his elbows, his body shaking as the man began to move in and out of him.

Mere feet away from where Ricardo, Jamie and Darren stood, transfixed, was Karen herself, magnificent in figure-sculpting black leather, and brandishing a many-tailed whip. The man kneeling in front of her was naked, and masturbating furiously as she wielded the whip across his upturned buttocks. His angular features were transformed into a picture of anguished bliss.

'Gunter?' Jamie breathed, his disbelief echoing that of Ricardo and Darren.

At that moment, a movement at the front of the building caught Ricardo's eye.

'Oh hell,' he breathed, 'Get back – quickly, through the rear door.'

Jamie and Darren obeyed as if on automatic pilot, stunned by the scenes of depravity they had just witnessed. Nothing they had imagined had even come close to the reality of what went on at Angels.

Ricardo hauled them around to the front of the building, and back into the shelter of the Bar del

Amore just as the women in Angels realised, too late, what was going on.

'Bloody hell, it's a police raid!' Darren said as he realised what was happening.

Ricardo nodded, watching grimly as Maria, Anita and Karen were hauled bodily from the building, and manhandled into the waiting van.

'Yes,' Ricardo said, grimly. 'I don't think we need worry about Angels any more.'

Sensing Darren's and Jamie's eyes on him, he realised that their first thought was that it was he who had phoned the police. No doubt Maria, Anita and Karen would think the same thing. He shook his head.

'It wasn't me,' he said.

'What are you going to do about it?' Darren asked.

'And what about Gunter and Ronan?' Jamie added, his normally healthy complexion looking grey.

Ricardo sighed heavily. 'Gunter and Ronan both seemed to be happy enough – did they look like prisoners to you?' Seeing their doubtful expressions, he sighed heavily. 'I will sort it out, somehow. But I think it might do them all good to – how do you say it? – stew a little first, don't you think?'

The three men grinned at each other and went to order a pint each from Pedro, who was quietly dozing on his feet behind the bar.

Chapter Eleven

'*L*et us out of here, immediately!'

Karen turned away from the door of the cell, only to find two pairs of wide, frightened eyes looking to her for guidance. Suppressing her own sense of panic, she attempted a wry smile.

'Come on, girls – it can't be that bad, can it?' she said.

Maria looked doubtful. 'The laws here are not so lenient as they are in England, Karen. What are we going to do?'

'I – ' Karen gritted her teeth. ' – I really don't have a clue. I didn't expect this to happen. I'm so sorry.'

She sank down on the cold, hard bench at the back of the cell and stared at the floor. She had never felt more miserable in her life.

'Don't worry, Karen,' Anita said, after a few minutes. 'It's not that we blame you – after all, we're in this together, aren't we? I suppose Maria and I were hoping you might have more of an idea of how to get out of this kind of mess than we have.'

Karen managed a weak smile. 'Sorry. I've never actually been arrested before.

'I could ring Ricardo,' Maria offered, her voice small.

'Absolutely not!' Anita and Karen said together.

Maria shrugged. 'Bad idea. Sorry.'

Karen smiled at her. 'You could telephone your uncle's lawyer, though – he might know someone who could help get us out of here.'

Maria nodded. 'As soon as someone comes, I'll ask for a telephone. They can't deny me that – can they?'

The others shook their heads without conviction. It was cold in the cell and each of the women was still wearing her skimpy stage costume. Inside the cell there were four bunks, each with a thin pillow and a threadbare blanket. As the hours ticked by, Karen huddled under her blanket and considered her position. After a while she dozed fitfully, and her sleep was peopled by nightmare figures who loomed at her in the darkness.

When morning arrived, they were woken by the banging of three tin plates through the hatch by the floor. They couldn't bring themselves to eat the dry, slightly stale bread roll, which seemed to constitute their breakfast.

After a few minutes, a policeman stopped outside the cell. His eyes passed lasciviously over the scantily clad women, his gaze settling on the chiffon covered fuzz between Maria's thighs. Without taking his eyes off it, despite her attempt to cross her legs and hide it, he said, 'Which one of you is Senorita Karen?'

'I am,' Karen said, stepping forward boldly.

The man's eyes flickered over her. 'This way,' he said curtly, unlocking the door.

Glancing quizzically at Maria and Anita, Karen stepped through the open door and followed the man along the corridor. She felt uncharacteristically self-conscious of her outlandish outfit as she walked through the public area of the police station, and all eyes followed her progress.

Though her Spanish was passably good, she was unable to follow the rapid-fire speech of the officer who appeared to be lecturing her across the desk. He gestured several times towards her, then nodded towards the door. Turning, Karen saw that Ricardo was lounging in the doorway, watching her.

'What do you want?' she asked baldly.

'The officer was just explaining – you have been released into my care. I have paid your bail money, but in return, the courts have decided you must live with me until your hearing.'

'What? You can't pull a stunt like that, Ricardo! I won't come with you.'

Ricardo shrugged. 'OK. Perhaps then, you would prefer to stay in your cell for a few more nights until the magistrate is due in Leventos?'

He began to turn away, but Karen stopped him. 'Wait! What . . . what about the others?'

'Maria and Anita will be taken care of.'

'What do you mean? By whom?'

'That is not your concern. All you need to know is that they will be released shortly. You should know, too, that their freedom is dependent on your behaviour.'

Karen stared at him, certain that she had never hated him more than she did at that moment.

'I have no choice but to come with you, do I?' she said through gritted teeth.

Ricardo seemed unperturbed by her anger. 'It would seem that way.'

'You arranged things like this.'

'Perhaps. Come.'

Every instinct in Karen told her to tell him to go to hell, but the thought of Maria and Anita spending another night in that filthy cell, never mind herself . . .

'All right,' she agreed, grudgingly.

Again she could feel dozens of pairs of eyes on her as she walked across the lobby and out into the bright sunshine. Ricardo's car was parked in the no parking zone directly outside the door, and he held open the passenger door for her. Karen sank into the soft, fragrant leather seat and waited for him to fire the engine.

They drove in silence, for Karen could not trust herself to speak, and Ricardo seemed disinclined to do so. As soon as she arrived at his house, Karen asked him if she could use the bathroom.

'Of course,' he replied, behaving like a perfect gentleman. 'I'll find you something clean to wear.'

Karen spent a long time under a warm shower, scrubbing away the smell of the prison from her skin. Her black leather basque and thigh-high boots looked strangely incongrous against the pristine white tiling in Ricardo's bathroom, and she was glad to peel them off. When she emerged from the shower, it was to find that he had left her an oversized white shirt made soft by countless launderings, and knee-high marl socks which crumpled into soft creases around her calves.

He smiled approvingly at her as she joined him in the kitchen, her short hair still wet and her skin, free of make-up, glowing pinkly where she had scrubbed it.

'That's better,' he said, running his eyes down the lean length of her brown-skinned legs.

Karen scowled darkly at him. 'You can keep your eyes to yourself. I never dreamt you would stoop so low as to report your own sister to the authorities!'

Ricardo regarded her calmly. 'The police raid had nothing to do with me,' he told her truthfully.

Karen eyes narrowed. 'You expect me to believe that?'

He shrugged. 'You can believe what you like, it happens to be the truth.'

Karen stared at him across the kitchen. His eyes were narrowed, his expression inscrutable, but she had the feeling that he was levelling with her.

'Why did you come and bail me out of gaol?' she asked curiously.

Ricardo looked away, busying himself with making coffee.

'I think you know why,' he said.

Karen felt as though the air in the room had stilled. It was very quiet, so quiet that it was possible to hear the gentle hiss and sigh of the sea on the beach below, and the occasional call of a sea bird as it wheeled past the kitchen window. She felt a warmth creeping through her veins which had little to do with the heat of the day, and everything to do with the man who was now staring at her, his dark eyes intense, reflecting her need.

'Ricardo – '

'Karen – '

They smiled faintly at each other as they both spoke at once. Then, as if obeying some inner, unspoken instinct, they moved towards each other, meeting in the middle of the cold, tiled floor.

'Ricardo, I – '

'Ssh!' he said, placing his hand over her mouth and drawing her towards him. 'Don't say anything. Too many words come between us . . .'

As he spoke, his warm breath brushed Karen's lips, and she found herself leaning into him, wanting to feel the heat and strength of his body close to hers.

There was something about Ricardo that made her feel weak, vulnerable in a way that appalled her as much as it thrilled her. Needing to assert herself, to establish some kind of control, she took the initiative, meshing her fingers in his hair and pulling his head down towards hers.

Their lips ground together, their teeth clashing as Karen kissed him aggressively, wanting – needing – to make her mark on him. Ricardo resisted, pulling away from her and bending her over the kitchen table, so that she was lying on her back, glaring up at him.

It was a large, sturdy table. Karen's legs hung down, her feet just above the floor as Ricardo covered her upper body with his.

'Don't you ever, ever try that with me!' he said, his eyes blazing at her.

Karen stared up at him and knew, beyond a doubt, that this man would never appreciate the particular pleasures to which she was able to introduce him. The thought gave her a pang of regret.

'You should keep an open mind,' she said, in spite of herself. 'You might find you enjoy the responsibility being taken away from you – oh!'

Ricardo pulled her arms up, above her head, and pinned them there with one large hand around her wrists. His body held her prisoner against the table and his legs trapped hers as he stood astride her.

'You push me too far, Karen,' he said, his jaw rigid with barely leashed anger. 'You always could.'

Karen gasped as, with his free hand, he pulled the two halves of her shirt apart. Buttons flew off it in all directions, but Ricardo was oblivious, his eyes feasting on her heaving, naked breasts and the uptilted, nut-hard discs of her nipples as they pointed accusingly towards him.

With a cry halfway between triumph and surrender, he lowered his head to them, sucking each little puckered promontory into his mouth in turn. Karen writhed as the sharp needles of pleasure-pain turned inward, arrowing towards the centre of her womb. She cried out as it cramped, the muscles contracting and relaxing as fresh moisture was expelled from between her swelling labia.

Ricardo seemed to be totally unaware of her

whimpering: he was focused solely on the trembling of her flesh beneath his lips. He made love to her as though he felt that her future desire for him depended solely upon his performance now, his lips moving across the surface of her skin with such precision that Karen soon felt as if every centimetre of her was aflame.

She wriggled beneath him, wanting to meet him on equal terms, but Ricardo would not let her go. Instead, his mouth moved lower, across the stretched plane of her belly, seeking the moist warmth of her most intimate flesh.

As his lips parted her outer labia and his tongue delved into the cleft, Karen cried out, her body jerking as if an electric current had passed through it. He let go of her arms then, so that he could use his hands to part the tender folds of flesh, though he sought the most sensitive path with his tongue.

Karen's hands wound themselves into his thick, dark hair, and she pressed his face against her open sex, desperate to feel the rasp of his tongue against her burgeoning clitoris. At the first touch she came, crying out as wave after wave of liquid heat flooded her senses.

Ricardo rose and, after unfastening his jeans, he spread her thighs apart so that his erect cock butted against the open portal of her sex. As her climax receded, he pushed his way into her body, feeling her hot, silky flesh enclose and caress him as her long legs wound themselves around his back.

Karen felt as though he was burning a path into her, he felt so hot as he thrust into her body. Pulling him against her with her heels, she wrapped her arms around him and levered herself up, so that she could watch his face as he came.

It was something she had never forgotten; the way his face went blank and his eyes glazed as every part of his attention focused on the sensations centralised in his loins. Ricardo did not disappoint her. With a low, juddering sigh, he poured his seed into her body, crushing her against him as he did so, as if he was desperate to stamp his mark of possession upon her.

Karen clung to him, her inner flesh convulsing in an echo of her orgasm as Ricardo's cock throbbed hotly inside her. Their lips met and they kissed blindly, all emotion conveyed through their touch without the need for words.

After a few minutes they disengaged, moving by unspoken consent to the master bedroom. The gloomy, wood-pannelled room was dominated by a huge four-poster bed, heavily carved with nameless creatures which looked as though they had risen from the pit of hell. Karen barely noticed as she clambered on to the bed, eager to touch and taste Ricardo, to reactivate his desire.

She wanted all of him, to enclose and surround him, and to drive him wild with desire so that he no longer knew where he was. Having dragged off the remains of the shirt and pulled the socks from her feet, she undressed him, her fingers feverish as they fumbled with buttons and zips and elastic, eager to feel the warm silk of his naked skin against her fingertips.

He was hot, his skin slick with sweat as she licked a path across his chest and down his midline. Circling his navel, she pushed him down on to the bed, so that he was lying on his back and she was crouched over him, her smooth, rounded buttocks pushed high in the air as she concentrated on the task she had set herself.

His penis was soft and warm and tasted of her feminine honey. Karen used her lips and tongue to tease and coax him back to full hardness again. When he was ready, she straddled him, guiding the tip of his cock to the gateway to her body and sinking down on him, drawing him inside her as deeply as she could, and wincing slightly as the bulb of his penis knocked against the entrance to her womb.

'Karen . . .' he whispered as she began to ride him, his large, brown hands reaching up to tweak and roll her nipples, squeezing the soft globes of her breasts so that the white flesh bulged out a little between his fingers.

Karen murmured incoherently, unable to formulate a single rational thought as the heat began to fill her, little feathers of pleasure playing up and down her spine. Ricardo reached between their two bodies and found her exposed clitoris with his thumb. He spread the thick, warm moisture which seeped from her over the button-hard nub of flesh, then moved it back and forth under the skin, creating a friction which echoed throughout her body, travelling through every nerve, every sinew and every tiny blood vessel, as if it was seeking an outlet, a way to disperse the sexual tension which gripped them.

It was impossible for Karen to hold back any

longer. She gripped Ricardo's hips with her knees, arching her back and allowing her head to tip back as her orgasm broke. Ricardo's hands spanned her waist, the fingers digging almost painfully into her soft flesh as her climax triggered his and their merged sex-flesh convulsed in unison.

Cresting, Karen fell forward, across Ricardo's body, and then they rolled over on to their sides, lying face to face as the last tremors died away.

'God Almighty,' he whispered, after a moment or two. 'What happened?'

Karen smiled, the action taking up the last of her depleted energy. 'It was good, wasn't it?'

Ricardo's eyes darkened and, once again, his fingers tightened on her waist, making her wince.

'It always was,' he said, his voice low and urgent, 'With us, it will always be good.'

Something in his tone alerted Karen to the seriousness of his mood, and she gazed solemnly at him.

'Is it like this for you when you have a man grovelling at your feet like a dog?' he asked her fiercely.

It seemed to Karen that anything other than the truth would be a travesty, a betrayal of the pleasure they had just shared. 'No,' she answered, truthfully. 'It has only ever been like this with you.'

His cock slipped quietly out of her body and he drew her into his arms. 'Then you must marry me – you know I will make you happy.'

Karen stiffened. '*Marry* you? You're joking, of course!'

'Why would I make jokes about something that important?'

Karen stared at him, and realised he *was* serious. She wanted to say that it was only sex, that he was reading too much into what had merely been a physical encounter, but she couldn't bring herself to do so. Somehow, to say such a thing would be to sell her own feelings short as well as his, and she simply couldn't do it.

There would be time enough to talk sensibly to him later, she reasoned. For now, all she wanted to do was sleep, lying contentedly in the warm circle of his arms . . .

Maria and Anita came to the house that night, bringing welcome news.

'All the charges have been dropped,' Anita said, relief written clearly over her face.

Karen, dressed once more in one of Ricardo's shirts and nothing else, raised her eyebrows, not daring to believe it was true.

'Dropped? How come?'

Anita glanced towards the doorway, through which the low murmur of voices could be heard as Ricardo and Maria talked in the kitchen.

'Aaron – he somehow managed to square everything. Amazing what you can do when you have oodles of cash, isn't it? He won't be able to build his hotel now, of course, and Angels has been closed, but it looks like we're all off the hook.'

Karen shook her head. 'I don't believe it! Where's Aaron now?'

Anita laughed. 'Oh, he caught the next available

flight back to London. I think the kitchen got just a little bit too hot for him, and he decided to get out while he still could!'

Karen laughed, not in the least bit bothered that he had left without trying to say goodbye.

'What about the others?' she asked. 'Ronan, Gunter, Adrian, Peter – '

'I've seen to it they've got somewhere to stay,' Anita reassured her.

Both Karen and Anita looked up as Ricardo appeared in the doorway. He was holding four glasses and Maria moved past him with a bottle of champagne.

'Let's drink to freedom, shall we?' she said thankfully.

Opening the bottle with a discreet 'pop', Ricardo poured them each a drink and they raised their glasses in a toast.

'To freedom,' all four said, though the three women said it more earnestly than Ricardo, who regarded them all with amusement.

'What will you do now?' he asked Anita. 'Will you go back home, to your job in England?'

Anita made a face at him. 'I don't think so.' She glanced at Maria, and the other girl reached for her hand.

'Anita and I have plans,' she said, never taking her eyes from her lover's face.

'Oh?' Karen said. 'What kind of plans?'

'The business kind,' Anita replied with a smile. 'We decided that Angels was a pretty good idea, despite the fact that we came to grief in the end. It was your idea, Karen, so we hope you'll join in.'

'Go on – I'm intrigued!' Karen said, sipping her champagne as Anita continued.

'Well, we'd like to open up again in new premises. Would you be interested in joining us?'

Karen grimaced. 'I don't have the capital for that kind of venture. Don't forget, the original Angels was set up for a certain timespan, and we had Aaron's investment to keep us going. I don't have that kind of money.'

'No, but I do.'

Everyone looked at Maria as she spoke, Anita proudly, since she knew exactly what Maria had done, the others quizzically.

'Uncle Julio left me his house in the mountains – it is perfect for what we have in mind, isn't it, Anita?'

Anita nodded, giving Maria's hand a squeeze. 'Perfect. Do say you'll join us, Karen. We had such fun!'

Karen smiled. 'We did, didn't we?' Glancing at Ricardo, she saw that he was watching her, guardedly. She had, thankfully, managed to talk him out of marriage, but she had no desire to leave him just yet.

'I can't join you, though I'm flattered that you've asked me.'

'How can we do it without you, Karen?' Maria wailed, clearly disappointed.

'Anita learns fast – together you'll make a success of it, I'm sure.' She turned to Ricardo and smiled at him. 'I have a project of my own,' she said softly, 'and it's going to take up a great deal of my time.'

Ricardo smiled and drew her closer to him so that he could kiss her.

'Sorry, ladies,' he said to Maria and Anita, 'but I claim exclusive rights to Karen from now on. Let me get more champagne from the fridge.'

Karen watched him go before turning back to her friends. They raised their eyebrows at the gleam in her eye.

'There's more than one way to subdue a man,' she said softly. 'I'll let him think he's won for now.'

The look of relief on Anita's face made Karen smile.

'For a moment there, I thought you'd given up!' Anita said, drawing Maria closer to her.

Karen laughed. 'Never!' she whispered. 'And the beauty of it is, he'll never know what hit him!'

The three women laughed and, when Ricardo came back into the room, they held their champagne glasses out together.

'Another toast, ladies?' he asked.

Karen caught Anita's and Maria's eye and saw that they were as amused as she was by Ricardo's cool, masculine self-assurance.

'To the Avenging Angels,' she said, raising her glass. 'God help all those who cross their path.'

Maria giggled, and she and Anita chinked their glasses against Karen's.

'Avenging Angels!' they cried.

Ricardo smiled at them, knowing that, now he had tamed Karen, he could afford to be indulgent.

'Ladies,' he murmured, raising his glass, relieved that, at last, he was able to relax in the company of the woman he loved.

BLACK LACE NEW BOOKS

Published in April

PALAZZO
Jan Smith

Disenchanted following her divorce, Claire Savage, a successful young advertising executive, finds her sexuality reawakened by the mysterious Stuart MacIntosh, whom she meets on a holiday in Venice. Stuart encourages her to explore the darkest reaches of erotic experience but, at the same time, draws her into a sensual intrigue involving one of his rich clients and Claire's best friend, the feisty Cherry. To complicate matters, Claire's ex-husband appears on the scene, leaving Claire not knowing who to trust.

ISBN 0 352 33156 9

THE GALLERY
Fredrica Alleyn

Jaded with her dull but secure relationship, WPC Cressida Farleigh agrees to take part in the undercover investigation of a series of art frauds which will separate her from her long-term boyfriend. The chief suspect is the darkly attractive owner of a London art gallery, and Cressida must use her powers of seduction in order to find out the truth. She encounters a variety of fascinating people, including a charming artist specialising in bizarre, erotic subject matter, and is forced to face up to the truth about her innermost desires.

ISBN 0 352 33148 8

Published in May

AVENGING ANGELS
Roxanne Carr

Disillusioned by the chauvinistic attitude of men in the idyllic summer resort of Tierra del Sol, tour guide Karen puts her fledgling skills as a dominatrix to the test. Pleasantly surprised by the results, Karen opens a bar – Angels – where women can realise their most erotic fantasies. However, the one man Karen really wants – Ricardo Baddeiras – the owner of a rival bar and brother of her business partner Maria, refuses to be drawn into her web of submission. Quite clearly, Karen will have to fine-tune her skills.

ISBN 0 352 33147 X

THE LION LOVER
Mercedes Kelly

It's the 1920s. When young doctor Mathilde Valentine becomes a medic in a mission in Kenya she soon finds out all is not what it seems. For one thing, McKinnon, the handsome missionary, has been married twice – and both of his wives have mysteriously disappeared. Mathilde falls for a rugged game warden but ignores his warnings that she might be in danger. Abducted and sold into slavery, she finds herself in the weird and wonderful harem of an Arabian sultan and discovers the truth about the two Mrs McKinnons. Will she regain her freedom?

ISBN 0 352 33162 3

PAST PASSIONS
An Anthology of Erotic Writing by Women
Edited by Kerri Sharp
£6.99

This is the second of the two larger format Black Lace anthologies – *Modern Love* being the first. While *Modern Love* is a selection of extracts from contemporary Black Lace novels, *Past Passions* is an inspired collection of excerpts taken from tales set in a variety of countries, cultures and centuries giving the reader the added pleasure of detail essential in the creating of historical settings.

ISBN 0 352 33159 3

To be published in June

JASMINE BLOSSOMS
Sylvie Ouellette

When Joanna is sent on a business trip to Japan, she expects nothing unusual. She soon finds that her sensuality is put to the test as enigmatic messages are followed by singular encounters with strangers who seem to know her every desire. She is constantly aroused but never entirely sated. As she gradually gives in to the magic of Japan – its people and its ways – she learns that she is becoming involved in a case of mistaken identity, erotic intrigue and mysterious seduction.

ISBN 0 352 33157 7

PANDORA'S BOX 2
An Anthology of Erotic Writing by Women
Edited by Kerri Sharp
£5.99

This is the second of the Pandora's Box anthologies of erotic writing by women. The book includes extracts from the best-selling and most popular titles of the Black Lace series, as well as four completely new stories. *Pandora's Box 2* is a celebration of four years of this revolutionary imprint. The diversity of the material is a testament to the many facets of the female imagination. This is unashamed erotic indulgence for women.

ISBN 0 352 33151 8

If you would like a complete list of plot summaries of Black Lace titles, please fill out the questionnaire overleaf or send a stamped addressed envelope to:-

Black Lace, 332 Ladbroke Grove, London W10 5AH

BLACK LACE BACKLIST

All books are priced £4.99 unless another price is given.

---------✂-------------------

Please send me the books I have ticked above.

Name   ....

Address ....

         ....

         ....

         .... Post Code   ....

Send to: **Cash Sales, Black Lace Books, 332 Ladbroke
Grove, London W10 5AH.**

Please enclose a cheque or postal order, made payable to
Virgin Publishing Ltd, to the value of the books you
have ordered plus postage and packing costs as follows:

   UK and BFPO – £1.00 for the first book, 50p for each
subsequent book.

   Overseas (including Republic of Ireland) – £2.00 for
the first book, £1.00 each subsequent book.

If you would prefer to pay by VISA or ACCESS/
MASTERCARD, please write your card number and
expiry date here:

....

Please allow up to 28 days for delivery.

Signature   ....

---------✂-------------------

BLACK
lace

WE NEED YOUR HELP...
to plan the future of women's erotic fiction –

– and no stamp required!

Yours are the only opinions that matter.

Black Lace is the first series of books devoted to erotic fiction by women for women.

We intend to keep providing the best-written, sexiest books you can buy. And we'd appreciate your help and valued opinion of the books so far. Tell us what you want to read.

THE BLACK LACE QUESTIONNAIRE

SECTION ONE: ABOUT YOU

1.1 Sex *(we presume you are female, but so as not to discriminate)*
   Are you?
   Male   ☐
   Female   ☐

1.2 Age
   under 21   ☐   21–30   ☐
   31–40   ☐   41–50   ☐
   51–60   ☐   over 60   ☐

1.3 At what age did you leave full-time education?
   still in education   ☐   16 or younger   ☐
   17–19   ☐   20 or older   ☐

1.4 Occupation _____

1.5 Annual household income

        under £10,000   ☐   £10–£20,000   ☐
        £20–£30,000   ☐   £30–£40,000   ☐
        over £40,000   ☐

1.6 We are perfectly happy for you to remain anonymous;
    but if you would like to receive information on other
    publications available, please insert your name and
    address

    _____

    _____

    _____

    _____

SECTION TWO: ABOUT BUYING BLACK LACE BOOKS

2.1 How did you acquire this copy of *Avenging Angels*?

        I bought it myself   ☐   My partner bought it   ☐
        I borrowed/found it   ☐

2.2 How did you find out about Black Lace books?

        I saw them in a shop   ☐
        I saw them advertised in a magazine   ☐
        I saw the London Underground posters   ☐
        I read about them in _____
        Other _____

2.3 Please tick the following statements you agree with:

        I would be less embarrassed about buying Black
        Lace books if the cover pictures were less explicit ☐
        I think that in general the pictures on Black
        Lace books are about right   ☐
        I think Black Lace cover pictures should be as
        explicit as possible   ☐

2.4 Would you read a Black Lace book in a public place – on
    a train for instance?

        Yes   ☐   No   ☐

SECTION THREE: ABOUT THIS BLACK LACE BOOK

3.1 Do you think the sex content in this book is:
        Too much   ☐   About right   ☐
        Not enough   ☐

3.2 Do you think the writing style in this book is:
        Too unreal/escapist   ☐   About right   ☐
        Too down to earth   ☐

3.3 Do you think the story in this book is:
        Too complicated   ☐   About right   ☐
        Too boring/simple   ☐

3.4 Do you think the cover of this book is:
        Too explicit   ☐   About right   ☐
        Not explicit enough   ☐

Here's a space for any other comments:

SECTION FOUR: ABOUT OTHER BLACK LACE BOOKS

4.1 How many Black Lace books have you read?   ☐

4.2 If more than one, which one did you prefer?

4.3 Why?

SECTION FIVE: ABOUT YOUR IDEAL EROTIC NOVEL

We want to publish the books you want to read – so this is your chance to tell us exactly what your ideal erotic novel would be like.

5.1   Using a scale of 1 to 5 (1 = no interest at all, 5 = your ideal), please rate the following possible settings for an erotic novel:

Medieval/barbarian/sword 'n' sorcery ☐
Renaissance/Elizabethan/Restoration ☐
Victorian/Edwardian ☐
1920s & 1930s – the Jazz Age ☐
Present day ☐
Future/Science Fiction ☐

5.2   Using the same scale of 1 to 5, please rate the following themes you may find in an erotic novel:

Submissive male/dominant female ☐
Submissive female/dominant male ☐
Lesbianism ☐
Bondage/fetishism ☐
Romantic love ☐
Experimental sex e.g. anal/watersports/sex toys ☐
Gay male sex ☐
Group sex ☐

Using the same scale of 1 to 5, please rate the following styles in which an erotic novel could be written:

Realistic, down to earth, set in real life ☐
Escapist fantasy, but just about believable ☐
Completely unreal, impressionistic, dreamlike ☐

5.3   Would you prefer your ideal erotic novel to be written from the viewpoint of the main male characters or the main female characters?

Male ☐   Female ☐
Both ☐

5.4 What would your ideal Black Lace heroine be like? Tick as many as you like:

Dominant	☐	Glamorous	☐
Extroverted	☐	Contemporary	☐
Independent	☐	Bisexual	☐
Adventurous	☐	Naïve	☐
Intellectual	☐	Introverted	☐
Professional	☐	Kinky	☐
Submissive	☐	Anything else?	☐
Ordinary	☐	_____	

5.5 What would your ideal male lead character be like? Again, tick as many as you like:

Rugged	☐		
Athletic	☐	Caring	☐
Sophisticated	☐	Cruel	☐
Retiring	☐	Debonair	☐
Outdoor-type	☐	Naïve	☐
Executive-type	☐	Intellectual	☐
Ordinary	☐	Professional	☐
Kinky	☐	Romantic	☐
Hunky	☐		
Sexually dominant	☐	Anything else?	☐
Sexually submissive	☐	_____	

5.6 Is there one particular setting or subject matter that your ideal erotic novel would contain?

_____

SECTION SIX: LAST WORDS

6.1 What do you like best about Black Lace books?

_____

6.2 What do you most dislike about Black Lace books?

_____

6.3 In what way, if any, would you like to change Black Lace covers?

_____

6.4 Here's a space for any other comments:

_____

_____

_____

_____

_____

Thank you for completing this questionnaire. Now tear it out of the book – carefully! – put it in an envelope and send it to:

> **Black Lace**
> **FREEPOST**
> **London**
> **W10 5BR**

No stamp is required if you are resident in the U.K.